The lights in the ice rink dimmed. "This is a couples skate," the announcer said. "So, find a partner."

I was busy helping Susan and Marcy get into rhythm when I felt a tap on my shoulder.

"Do you need a partner?" Nick asked.

I turned around and looked into his beautiful blue eyes. I was glad it was dark inside, because I knew that I was blushing. He took my hand gently.

"I'm Nick. And you're Linda Jean, right?"

"Yes," I managed to say as he led me out into the stream of skaters.

**Look for these other books in
The Forever Friends Club series:**

Friends Save The Day!

Cindy Savage

Cover illustration by Richard Kriegler

To Louise Johnson—
for reading even those that aren't published

Published by Willowisp Press, Inc.
401 E. Wilson Bridge Road, Worthington, Ohio 43085

Printed in the United States of America
10 9 8 7 6 5 4 3 2 1

ISBN 0-87406-422-8

One

AMBER Quick's basement game room had been transformed into a wild jungle. Large, lifelike cutouts of wild animals covered the walls, and green and purple streamers twisted from the center of the room to the four corners. Big tan and green balloons hung from the ceiling and lay scattered around the floor. There was even carnival music playing in the background.

"Watch this," I said to the group of wide-eyed six year olds. "Up, Mascot. Now, speak."

Mascot, my golden retriever, raised up on his back legs and let out two sharp barks. I gave him a dog biscuit as his reward for doing the trick.

"Wow, Linda Jean. That was really neat. Can I try to do it, too?" Amber asked. "Would Mascot do a trick for me?"

"Sure," I told the little birthday girl. She looked so cute all dressed up in her red velvet dress. "Come over here, and hold this hoop for me. That will be a big help."

Amber walked over to me excitedly and took the large hoop in her hand. She held the hoop as far away from her body as she could.

"Okay, Amber, now tell him to jump. Say 'jump, Mascot, jump,'" I told her.

Amber smiled at my dog, who weighed about 60 pounds more than she did. "Jump, Mascot. Jump!" she yelled at him.

But Mascot just sat there.

"Maybe you could say it again a little bit louder this time. Mascot has to know that it's an order," I explained.

Amber yelled the commands again as loudly as she could. I dangled a biscuit in front of the hoop to give Mascot some incentive to jump. And he did. He neatly made it through the hoop, and Amber jumped up and down excitedly.

Her audience laughed and clapped.

"Okay, everybody," I said. "Let's eat the cake."

"Hey, that was a great job, Linda Jean,"

Aimee said as we helped the kids wash their hands. "The kids loved the circus animal theme today. But it seemed you had to do more than your share for this party. Why don't you take a break while the rest of us give out the refreshments?"

"Forget it," I said. "The party is far from over. Joy still has to do her jungle dance. And Krissy's clown act is coming up. Besides, we're in Party Time together. I'll just wait and take a break afterward with you guys."

All this talk about parties and jobs may sound confusing, but it's really quite simple. I'm Linda Jean Jacobs, and I live on Honeybee Court with my friends, Aimee Lawrence, Kristina Branch, and Joy Marshall. We're The Forever Friends Club.

Our club meets at Joy's house every day after school. The three of them have met there ever since they were little. I joined in the tradition two and a half years ago when I moved to Atlanta, Georgia, with my father. Joy, Aimee, and Krissy made me feel welcome immediately. And now I often forget that I haven't been there forever, too.

Anyway, last summer The Forever Friends Club started a business called Party Time. We put on all kinds of parties for kids. We do birthday parties and skating parties, and we even entertain kids while their parents are at meetings. We also help Abby Marshall, Joy's mom, with her booming catering business.

I think the best parties are those where Abby does the catering and we do the entertaining. It's especially fun if it's an all-kid event—no grown-ups. We all work together and have an absolute blast.

"Hey, I thought you were going to help us get the food together," Aimee called.

I shook my head to clear it. "I'm sorry. I was just thinking about how Party Time got started. Do you know what I just realized? We've put on almost 50 parties now. Can you believe it?"

Aimee laughed. She said she thought it felt more like 75 parties. I joined my three business partners by the specially decorated birthday table. I poured the juice while Aimee served animal-shaped sandwiches. Joy gave each child a granola parfait with a cardboard tiger on top.

"That's fantastic," Krissy said when I repeated my discovery. "We should do something special to celebrate. Maybe we could throw a party just for ourselves."

"That's a great idea," Joy added. "Do you think we should have Abby cater it?"

"If I had a pillow in my hand right now, I'd throw it at your head," I teased her.

I looked over at Amber, who was jumping up and down. "Hurray! she yelled. "We're going to have a pillow fight."

"Hold on," I told her, gently pushing her back down in her seat. "I was only joking."

"Can I have more parfaits?" Amber's little brother, Christopher, asked, holding up his spoon.

"No. You have to save room for the giant pretzels," Joy said, wiping his face and grabbing his sticky paper plate at the same time. She gave him a smaller plate with a golden pretzel in the middle.

"Yummy," he said after his first bite. "This is fun."

"It's nice that so many kids have a good time at our parties," I told my friends later as we walked home. The party had been only three blocks away from Honeybee Court, so we had walked over.

I smiled at my friends. We made quite a picture as we carried all the supplies and cages of animals. We all looked different from each other. I have straight blondish hair that's just about at my shoulders. Krissy has really pretty blond hair that she wears in a ponytail a lot. Then there's Aimee and her dark skin and curly black hair, and Joy with her feathery haircut.

But as we walked down the street, nobody could have seen what we looked like. Each of us carried so much that our faces were hidden.

People definitely would have noticed the skunk, though. Saucy Skunk is my buddy. He was descented (that means his scent glands were moved so he can't spray anymore), but you can't tell that by looking at him. People usually panic whenever they see him.

"These cages sure are getting heavy," Krissy complained.

"Let's set them down and rest for a minute," I suggested. "We just have one block to go, anyway."

We put down the cages, leftover decorations, craft supplies, and costumes along the side of the road. As I lowered Saucy's cage, the latch came loose. The next thing we knew, Saucy was racing down the street and across the neighbors' lawns with Mascot at his heels.

The Turners were out in their front yard hanging up a tire swing for their son. "Look out. It's a skunk!" Mrs. Turner yelled, tripping over the toolbox on her way to the house.

We ran as fast as we could, trying to head Saucy and Mascot off wherever we could. But they were just too fast for us. We lept over hedges and dodged trees.

"Come back here!" I shouted. "Saucy, you come back here right now."

Three yards later, Mascot cornered Saucy against Mrs. Marlowe's picket fence. I ran to catch up with them. "Come on, Saucy," I coaxed. "Come to Linda Jean."

Saucy flipped his tail and dashed through the flower beds and the garden.

"Get that skunk out of my garden!" Mrs. Marlowe yelled at us from her kitchen window.

"We're trying, Mrs. Marlowe," Aimee told her.

"Well, try harder then. Stay out of my flowers. And if you don't catch him, I'm going to shoot him!" she yelled.

Until Mrs. Marlowe mentioned shooting, I had been slowly trying to coax Saucy out of the garden. But I would not let him be hurt by anybody. So, I jumped forward into the flower beds and grabbed him. "Get that stupid animal out of my sight," Mrs. Marlowe said from her front porch.

"We're going right now," I said. "We're sorry."

But she didn't hear me. She was too busy waving her BB gun and lecturing us on pet control and responsibility.

"You can't ever make pets of skunks," Mrs. Marlowe called out to us. "They'll always be wild animals. You know, the first chance they get, they'll escape."

I held on tightly to Saucy and grabbed Mascot's leash. Krissy and Joy ran back for the other cages and supplies.

"Let's get home quickly," I said. "She was so mean. I'd be happy if I didn't have to see her ever again."

"You don't have to," Joy said. "We can avoid her street. Just be sure to keep Saucy out of her yard."

"Don't worry. I will," I assured her.

A few minutes later, we were finally walking up the front steps to my house. A strange car with the county symbol on the side was parked in our driveway.

"I wonder what is going on," I wondered aloud.

The house was silent when I opened the door. *That's odd*, I thought. *The birds in my house aren't even singing.*

We put the cages down in the kitchen and then headed into the living room to find my father.

"Dad?" I called.

"I'm in here," he said.

"Hi, Dad. What's going on? The animals are so quiet."

"Linda Jean, I would like you to meet Jill Sinclair. She's with the county's animal control division. She is here to talk to you about your animals."

My throat tightened up, and my palms began to sweat. "Is something wrong?" I asked quickly.

She handed me an official-looking piece of paper, but she started to explain before I had a chance to read it.

"There has been a complaint about your animals," she said. "An anonymous caller reported that you were keeping too many animals in your yard, and that they made too much noise and smelled."

"I have licenses for all my pets," I protested. "And I clean their cages all the time. And they don't make too much noise."

"Miss Jacobs, your father just showed me all of your animals. I didn't find any violations of the city codes."

"So, then what's wrong? I don't understand."

"I do see that you take good care of your animals. Each has had its shots. And each one is licensed. I see no evidence of neglect or mistreatment on your part."

I nodded, waiting to hear the bad news. "Yes, I love my animals, and I'd never hurt them," I said.

"I know that," she said and smiled. "Would you sit down for a minute? Let me explain what this complaint means."

I sat down on the couch beside Dad. My friends sat down on the floor to listen.

"Whenever my office receives a complaint, even an anonymous one like this, it must be checked out. If we don't find any violations, we let everything go on as before."

"So, does that mean I can keep all my pets?" I asked.

"It means that you can keep them unless there are further complaints about them," she explained.

"But if I could just talk to the person who complained, I could tell them all about my animals and how special they are. I could tell them how I rescued my goose from a raccoon, and how Oswald the Owl is blind in one eye and runs into things if he tries to hunt at night."

"If it weren't for Linda Jean, most of these animals would be dead," Joy added. "If a stray animal is hurt or sick or abused, people know that Linda Jean will take great care of it. Isn't that what the animal control people care about?"

"I understand that Miss Jacobs is good with strays, but a complaint must be dealt with. I'm afraid that if you are reported again, you will have to find other homes for your animals or turn them over to the city."

After everyone had left, I cried on Dad's shoulder for a long time. He knew how much my animals meant to me.

"I don't know what I would do without my pets!" I said as I dried my eyes. "Dad, we'll just have to move to the country right away."

"Linda Jean, you know we can't do that," Dad said.

"Why not?" I asked. I couldn't believe that he didn't agree with me.

"That's not very practical, honey," he said. "Besides, then you would miss your friends."

I wiped away more tears. "I don't know which is worse. I can't believe it, Dad. Who would do this? Who has it in for me around here?"

He shrugged his shoulders, and then the answer came to me. I pictured Mrs. Marlowe standing on her front porch yelling at us. *Could she be the anonymous caller?*

Two

"WHAT are you going to do about your animals?" Aimee asked me the next morning. Krissy, Joy, and I had met at Aimee's house to walk to school together.

"I wish I knew what to do," I said as I stepped off Aimee's porch into the drizzle. Usually, I enjoyed walking in the rain and splashing in the puddles. But the cold, steady downpour only reminded me of Mandy, my adorable persian cat.

Mandy had been really funny that morning. While I was fixing breakfast, she stood by the back door and begged to go outside. But, when I finally opened the door, she wasn't very brave about facing the rain. She finally stepped onto the patio and did a crazy little cat dance. Mandy put one paw down at a time, and then she lifted it and shook the water off. It was step-shake-wiggle all the way down the sidewalk.

What if I have to give Mandy away? I thought. *I just can't do it. She's so lovable. And who would want a cat who is nearly deaf?*

Joy opened her umbrella. "Did you and your dad have any ideas last night after we left?"

"No, we didn't," I told her sadly. "Not one."

"Well, we have to do something," Joy said and then looked at the others. "We can't let some unknown complainer make Linda Jean give away her pets. It's just not fair."

Krissy's rubber raincoat squeaked as she walked down the sidewalk. She kept her head down as she watched out for the puddles.

"The first thing we need to do to solve this mystery is to find out who turned Linda Jean in," Krissy said. "I mean, if we could find out who reported her, then we could ask them to drop the complaint."

"Who could it be?" I asked. "It can't be Mr. Cobble next door. He has three dogs himself. And he brought presents for all of my pets on Christmas, so it can't be him."

"What about Mrs. Granger?" Joy suggested. "She doesn't have any pets."

"Yeah, but she's hardly ever home," Aimee added.

"And when she is," I added, "she asks how my parakeets are doing. I don't think she would report me."

Krissy kicked at a small stone and watched it roll down the street. "Then that leaves Mrs. Marlowe as a prime suspect," she said.

"Mrs. Marlowe must be the one," Joy agreed. "She really was upset at us for chasing Saucy through her yard yesterday. Do you think she would have called in to report you?"

I shook my head. "Jill Sinclair was already at my house when we got there. There's no way that Mrs. Marlowe could've complained that quickly. The call had to have been made earlier."

"It still could have been Mrs. Marlowe who complained," Krissy said.

We were almost to our school, Martin Luther King Junior High. It loomed ahead of us in the gray mist.

"Wow, that looks really cheery," I mumbled sarcastically, looking at the ground. As we walked across the grass, we could see Graham waiting for us on the school steps.

"What do you mean?" Aimee asked defensively. "Graham is always a cheery sight." She ran ahead to talk with Graham Moore, who is sort of her boyfriend. They spend a lot of time together, but they don't go on real dates or anything. They work together at WBCC, the local television station where Graham's mother produces a talk show that is hosted by Aimee's father.

"So, how's our honorary Forever Friends Club member this morning?" I heard Aimee ask him. We made Graham an honorary member after he came to our rescue and helped us with one of our parties. Graham is really terrific at card tricks and all kinds of zany jokes. The kids loved him at our party.

"Well, I'm pretty good. But I've been worried about Linda Jean's problem ever since I heard about it," Graham said, looking at me.

"How did you find out?" I asked.

"Aimee called me," he said.

"I thought Graham might have an idea that would help," Aimee said. "I thought his mother could produce a show about animals, featuring you, of course. She could show you as a responsible pet owner, and you could talk about what can be done to stop people who make complaints."

"That's a nice idea, but I don't think it would work," I said. "Who would be interested in my problem?"

Graham looked thoughtful for a moment. "Hey, I don't know about getting your problem on TV, but I do know a great place where your animals would be loved and well cared for. That is, if you do have to find other homes for them."

I looked up at him. I knew he was just trying to help, but I didn't want to face the horrible thought of giving away my pets.

"Graham, I really don't want to think about it," I said, attempting a smile.

"I understand. But just remember that I do have an idea that you might like," he said.

"I'll remember," I replied sadly.

I spent most of the day thinking about my pets, and remembering their funny expressions and their different personalities. They really are like a lot of the kids we put on parties for because they love attention and special treats. I knew all of my pets so well. I just couldn't imagine living without them.

I guess my love of animals comes from my parents. Although Mom and Dad are divorced, they work together at the Yerkes Institute, where animal behavior is closely studied. They even have chimps there that are great fun to play with. But visiting chimps wouldn't be the same as having pets at home. And our house just wouldn't be a home without the animal calls ringing in the air.

By the time school was over, I was exhausted from trying not to think about my problems and then thinking about them, anyway. We met at Joy's house for our daily Forever Friends Club meeting. The smells of won-ton filling and pork fried rice filled the air. My mouth watered just thinking about the rest of the meal—chicken chow mein with cashews and sweet-and-sour meatballs with pineapple chunks.

"I need something to keep my mind off my problems," I said as I pulled up a chair at the kitchen table. "Let's eat!"

"Let's wrap," Abby said with a grin, handing each of us a big tray with a stack of won-ton skins, a bowl of beaten egg white, and a spoon. She set a steaming bowl of filling (a mixture of bean sprouts, onions, mushrooms, and water chestnuts) in the middle of the table.

"Don't we even get to take a taste?" Joy

complained to Abby.

"Okay. How's this?" Abby asked, producing four plates with samples of each food on them.

"All right," Joy and I both said at once.

As soon as we polished off our plates full of food, we washed our hands, put on our hair nets, and began wrapping won-tons.

"We also need to plan the parties for this week," Abby said.

"What kind of cake does Susan Kopolas want for her skating party? Do you think Randall Williams' birthday guests would like dinosaur cookies?"

I took a spoonful of won-ton filling and placed it in the middle of the square noodle. Dipping my fingers in the egg, I wet the edges of the wrap and folded them up around the filling and sealed it carefully. I felt the tension easing from my shoulders as I slipped into the routine of stuffing, wrapping, and sealing.

"Okay, let's talk about Randall's party at the Junior Science Museum first," Aimee suggested. "Linda Jean, you've been there lots of times. What do they usually do for demonstrations? Will we have to help them do this part of the party?"

"It works like this," I said, my voice squeaking a little. "The kids will tour the museum's exhibits first. Then there's a really good area that shows animals in their natural habitats. In this area, there is also a demonstration of the food chain process."

"Are the animals real? I've never been there before," Krissy said. "I was wondering if the kids would get scared. I mean, Randall's friends are only seven."

I smiled. "No, there's nothing to scare them. Most of the animals are behind glass windows, and a few are in the open so they can be touched. They have a brown bear that was accidentally killed by a car. The museum had him stuffed, and now he sits in the lobby so the kids can feel his fur."

Just thinking about the live animals at the museum made me miss my pets at home. They weren't even gone, but I missed them, anyway. It was difficult to tell my friends about the museum animals while mine were sitting at home on probation. If my pets didn't stay quiet, they would be doomed. And I didn't want to think about that.

"I'm sure the kids will like the up close part

with the animals the best," I said. "One of the museum guides will have the kids sit in a circle in the room where all the live animals are kept. She'll bring in an owl, a small snake, and a few others for them to feel."

Abby took the finished trays of filled wontons off the table and set out more stacks of wraps and filling.

"I'll get some more egg," Joy offered.

"When and where can the kids eat at the museum?" Abby asked. "Yeah, do we have to bring tables?" Aimee added.

"Well, the museum has a special room that is already set up for parties. So, I guess all that we have to do is watch the kids enjoy the tour, and then serve the refreshments. It should be a breeze."

After another 30-minute discussion about Randall's party, most of the plans were decided on. Aimee decided to use fake fur as a covering for the party bags that the kids would make. She planned to have the children select their favorite animals and glue them to their prize bags. Joy had agreed to help Aimee with the crafts since there wasn't any room in the museum to perform a dance.

Krissy always dressed up her clown costume to fit the theme of the party. This time, she picked stuffed tiger tails as the perfect way to jungle-up her suit. She would hang them from her waist. She also picked a few of her newest clown tricks to perform for the kids.

That only left my portion of the party. My main job always involves showing off the animals. But for the first time, I was really dreading a party. I would give anything to stay home that day.

Three

WE spent the rest of the afternoon making plans for Susan Kopolas' skating party. We decided to meet at the ice rink one day after school to make sure that we all remembered how to skate. After all, it wouldn't look very professional to have the party hosts falling down on the ice in front of the kids.

I was relieved when our meeting finally ended. I was tired from trying to look happy all afternoon. I shook my umbrella out on the front porch of my house and then hung my coat in the entry hall to dry.

"Hi, Dad. How was your day?" I asked him as I walked into the living room.

"It was fine," he said. "I'm in the kitchen. I have a surprise for dinner. How does food from your favorite Chinese restaurant sound?

I stopped there on the way home."

I groaned. "Uh, Dad, it sounds great. But would you believe we just spent all afternoon cooking and eating Chinese food for Abby's catering job tomorrow? I'm really sorry." I held up my wrinkled fingertips. "These hands have wrapped no less than 300 won-tons since school let out today."

Dad laughed. "Okay, I get the idea. I'll put yours in the refrigerator, and you can heat it up when you're hungry."

"Thanks," I said, plopping down in a chair. "Maybe I'll heat it up for breakfast."

"You really seem tired today, honey," Dad observed.

"I am," I admitted. "I'm especially tired of worrying about complaining neighbors. All day, I've been worrying that the dogs will start howling at fire trucks, or that Percy, Mac, and Oswald are having a screeching match."

I told Dad about my classes at school. And he discussed his latest projects with the chimps at the institute. Finally, I brushed the folds out of my pants and stood up.

"Well, I guess I'd better feed all the animals so I can do my homework sometime tonight, too. There's a lot of work awaiting me."

"Please try not to worry too much, Linda Jean," Dad said. His voice sounded cheerful, but his eyes showed that he was worried, too. "Sometimes things have a way of working themselves out. Just wait and see, okay?"

I smiled in spite of everything, because he uses his favorite "wait and see" expression for everything that happens. And I knew that Dad was usually right about things like that. He's a strong believer in letting people and animals solve their own problems at their own pace.

It was the same advice Dad gave me when Mom and her new family moved to Atlanta last summer. I had been really afraid that she'd want me to move in with them. But after a while I discovered that Mom didn't want that at all. She really just wanted us to spend some time together to get to know each other again. And after I got to know my stepbrother, stepsister, and stepfather, I even liked them.

I guess Dad could be right again, I told myself as I began setting out the food dishes and filling them with food for each animal. Maybe the first complaint would be the last. Then there wouldn't be anything else to worry about. I sure hoped so.

"Good evening, Gunther," I said, petting my goose's long gray neck. "You're molting a little, I see." I looked at the handful of soft feathers that came off as I rubbed his back.

I filled Gunther's tray with cracked corn and vegetables. Our backyard is fenced in, so Gunther can wander around in the yard all day eating bugs. "I see you've been collecting rocks," I said, taking four rocks out of his cage and tossing them into the yard. Gunther is worse than a pack rat at collecting things.

Then I gave Percy and Mac dishes of parrot mix and some spare vegetables from the grocer down the street. He always saved the veggies that were leftover and about to spoil, and gave them to me once a week. He thought my unusual animals were interesting.

"What will happen to you two if you move to another home?" I asked them. "Will your new owners know what to feed you? Will they know that lettuce and celery are all water and no nutrients, and that they make you guys sick?"

"Up, up, and away," Mac squawked.

"Blow it out your ear," Percy added. Talking birds have minds of their own, especially if they had different owners before you. So, you never really know what they'll say next. It makes life kind of fun.

"Give me a kiss," I said to Percy.

"Give me a dollar," he said.

I handed him a small piece of carrot.

"Smack." He made a slurping kind of kissing sound near the bars of his cage. Then he reached over and tried to bite my lip.

"Hey, that's enough, you bad bird," I told him. "Now, eat your dinner like a good boy."

"Eat your dinner. Eat your dinner," Mac repeated over and over. I fed each of my pets and gave each of them some personal attention. I gave live crickets to Lucy, my iguana. Regina Rabbit ate alfalfa pellets and fruit. It was weird though that both Lucy and Regina had rocks in their cages, too. *Gunther must have been really busy to collect so many rocks*, I thought.

Saucy munched on leftover vegetables, nuts, and seeds. Skunks are scavengers, so they eat practically anything. I scratched her behind her ears. "No more escape artist tricks," I warned her playfully.

"How are you doing in there? Where's Taffy?" I asked Harry and Max, my turtles. "Oh, there you are," I said, picking up the little turtle that Krissy's little sister, Kitty, had given me. "Hey, are you ready for a little exercise?"

I lowered the container of goldfish and crickets into the turtles' tank. Harry quickly spotted the fish swimming around. His flippers poked out, and he scooted himself across the sand toward his dinner. I put the screen lid on the tank so the crickets couldn't jump out and went over to give Oswald the owl his mouse.

"Sorry, but I can't watch this," I told him as he blinked one sleepy eye at me and then stared hungrily at the mouse. "I love you, but I wish you ate hamburger."

I was so busy visiting with Susie the squirrel and her six babies that I didn't notice how late it was getting.

Suddenly, I heard the clock inside signal that it was 7:00. I scrambled to feed the rest of the animals, and then I ran up to my room to do my homework.

"Darn. Now, I'm going to have to stay up late to finish all of my homework," I said out loud. I spread my books out on the bed to see what assignments had to be done.

Dad walked by and peeked in a couple of times during the next two hours, but I didn't even look up. Seventh grade is so much harder than sixth grade. Instead of one teacher who gives you homework, you have six or seven teachers who think you have a spare hour for each of them every night.

I looked down my list of assignments and realized that I would need at least another four hours to complete them.

"How am I going to read four chapters in four subjects and still do three pages of math, and. . .oh, no!" I stared at my open Spanish book in front of me. The homework assignment lay on top.

"Examinacion mañana," I read. "That means test. I can't believe I have a test tomorrow. I completely forgot."

There was absolutely no way that I could study for a Spanish test. I was exhausted. There was no way that I'd remember a thing. I rolled over and set my alarm for 5:00 a.m.

I stacked my books on the floor, turned off the light, and fell asleep in my clothes. It seemed like only a minute later that the alarm went off. But then I realized it wasn't my alarm clock at all. It was Percival. He was squawking in his loudest voice.

Just as I sat up in bed, Mascot let out a

howl that would have awakened anything—
alive or dead. I glanced at the clock on my night
stand and saw that it was nearly 9:30. Dad
and I walked into the kitchen at the same time.
We both looked at each other with the same
panicked expressions.

"This is all we need," I said as we ran out
into the backyard. "Hush. Come on, you guys.
Now, shhh!"

The covers to their cages had fallen off with
all their swinging back and forth. I steadied
the cages and looked around for a raccoon or
some other reason why they all were making
such a fuss.

"I know why they are throwing fits," Dad
said suddenly.

Frightened, I turned to look at him. In one
hand, he was holding a rock. In the other, he
was holding Max, who had a chip freshly
knicked off the back of his shell.

"Oh, Max!" I cried, examining his shell. I
looked out at the yard, and there were at least
10 rocks scattered over the yard. These were
the same kind of rocks that I had blamed
Gunther for the night before. "Who would do
this?" I asked Dad.

"Whoever threw these rocks seems to mean

business," Dad said grimly. "They must want you to get rid of your pets. And they plan to help you do it."

"Dad, it's just not fair," I said. I could barely hold back the tears. "What kind of a person would hurt my animals? I mean, they aren't hurting anyone."

"I don't know, Linda Jean. But I do think that the Animal Control people should be looking for the person who is throwing the rocks. That's the real problem," he said angrily.

By the time we quieted the animals, repaired Max's shell, and cleaned up all the rocks, it was nearly 12:00.

The next morning I turned in the homework that I'd finished. But my Spanish test was a total loss. I flat out failed. I thought the day couldn't get any worse—until I went to science class.

Usually, I love Mr. Servey's science class. Actually, it's usually my favorite class of the day, but today we had to dissect frogs. And, the worst part about it was that the frogs were alive. They weren't the kind that had been stored for centuries at a laboratory. No, we were supposed to stick a long needle down their spinal cords and up into their brains to scramble them and kill the frog. Well, actually, the needle would just paralyze the frog and make it brain dead. Then we would cut the frogs open and watch their hearts beat.

I just couldn't do it. A girl has to draw the line somewhere. I looked at the frog, and I thought about Max and the rocks and all the cruelty that seemed to be everywhere. There was no way that I would add to that by killing a frog.

"Mr. Servey," I said, raising my hand. "May I talk with you a minute, please?"

"Sure, Linda Jean. What is it?" he asked as he walked over to my desk.

"I don't want to do the frog dissection," I told him. I guess I could have told him a few reasons why, but I just sat there waiting.

Mr. Servey laughed. "You're kidding me, right? After all, you're the most promising scientist in this room. I was counting on you to help the others with their frogs."

His smile faded as I shook my head. "I can't do it, Mr. Servey." I held up my squirming frog. "What has this little frog ever done to me, or to you? Did it ask to be raised in a lab and put to death for a simple experiment?"

Mr. Servey wasn't smiling now. He looked irritated and even kind of angry. "I never expected this out of you, Linda Jean. You have known for weeks that we were going to dissect a frog in class. Why did you wait until today to discuss this problem with me?"

I didn't want to talk about it any longer. I just wanted to go home and protect my animals. I wanted to make sure Max's shell was healing and that no more rocks were flying into our yard. I wanted to take home the frog and let him enjoy his life.

"I don't know why I waited. You can give me an *F* on the project," I told him. "But I won't do it!"

"You may spend the rest of science period in study hall," he said. "And Monday morning I want you to come to my office before school to discuss this matter in detail."

I gathered my books and left. Everyone in the class was staring at me, but I didn't care. In my hand, I clutched the frog that I had saved. I walked right by study hall and taped a note to Krissy's locker to tell her what had happened. Then I walked straight out the front door of the school and down the steps.

I knew I would get in trouble for that, too.

Four

"I still can't believe you just walked out of school yesterday," Krissy said Saturday morning. We were busy setting up all the tables and decorations for Randall Williams' party at the museum.

"I can't believe it myself," I told her. "I've never cut school before in my whole life."

"Maybe no one knows you did it. I mean, you were supposed to be in science class, not study hall. Do you think Mr. Servey called down to tell the study hall teacher you were on your way?"

"I honestly don't know. I don't know about anything anymore," I replied.

"Well, I do know that we have to pay attention to Randall's party. The guests are beginning to arrive now," Joy said.

"I'm sorry I'm so distracted," I said quickly.

"Hey, Linda Jean, you know that we're behind you all the way," Joy said with a smile. "We'll find out who is complaining and throwing the rocks. Then things will get back to normal."

"I sure hope you're right," I admitted. But I knew that just finding out who was complaining wouldn't solve the problem. Once I found out who it was, I would have to explain why I had so many animals. Then I would have to convince the person to drop the complaint against me.

My head was spinning. I thought again of Mrs. Marlowe. When I had walked home carrying the frog yesterday, she had glared at me from her living room window. As I looked back at her, I thought I saw her reach for the phone. I was more sure than ever that she was the one who had reported me. I needed to talk to her—and soon.

"Here come the kids," Aimee announced. "I'll hand out name tags since you will be getting the kids ready for the tour, Linda Jean."

For the first time that day, I really looked at the museum. On one wall, there was a beautiful dinosaur painting created by a local high school student. On another wall hung samples of different tree barks.

I gathered the kids together in front of the entrance to the environment room. A museum guide came over to join our group.

"Hi, I'm Kathy," she said to the group. "Before we go into the environment room, I'd like to show you a few things out here in the lobby."

Joy, Aimee, and Mrs. Williams joined the group of kids as Kathy showed them the table of rocks. "This is an obsidian needle," Kathy said, holding up a pointed piece of black shiny rock. "It was formed by a volcano. The needles are made by dripping lava that cools and hardens before it falls."

The kids picked up the different rocks as Kathy told a story about each one. I smiled as she explained that the Indians used soapstone dust for baby powder.

"Oh, that's gross," Randall said.

"And it's also used for war paint," Kathy added, taking her finger and rubbing it across the back of his hand.

Randall looked at the streak of reddish brown. "Oh, that's cool!" he exclaimed.

As we went into the environment room,

Krissy came up behind me.

"Are you feeling better?" she asked me.

"Yeah, I guess so. I'm just trying to keep my mind on today's party. But those rocks in the display cases keep reminding me about my animals. I just have to solve this mess," I said.

She grinned. "We will. Now, let's have fun. This is one of your favorite places, remember?"

The room was dark and exciting. We walked around and peeked into the lighted display areas. Kathy explained how the animals and plants lived in the mountain zone, the tundra zone, the forest, and the desert.

I was having a great time until I saw a stuffed skunk in one of the glass cases. The skunk looked just like Saucy. Kathy quickly pointed out that the stuffed animals had died naturally before they were brought to the museum for display. But that didn't help how I felt.

"Linda Jean, doesn't that skunk look real?" asked Calvin, a red-haired boy with cute freckles. "I'll bet I could really scare the girls at school if I had that skunk to carry around."

"Why would you want to do that?" I suddenly snapped at him.

"Because girls are fun to scare. They scream

and run and stuff." Calvin grinned. "Skunks are bad because they smell. Girls hate them."

I wasn't in the mood to hear mean remarks about skunks. "Listen, Calvin," I said. "Skunks only spray their enemies for protection. They're not bad animals at all. Every animal has a special way of keeping safe in the wild. Skunks would be more scared of you than you would be of them."

"But I don't stink," he said defensively.

"Maybe you do to a skunk," I told him.

"Says who?"

"Says me." I was beginning to get irritated. *Why was I getting into an argument with a seven year old?* I wondered. It was ridiculous. I tapped Aimee on the shoulder and asked if I could change sides with her.

I breathed a sigh of relief as she began talking with Calvin about the red spots on a flying blackbird's wings. I took a few minutes to look around the museum by myself. I had forgotten how many of the animals looked like my pets at home.

Then Kathy took the kids into the live animal room. I took three deep breaths and followed them in. *These kids need you to be strong and to be fun,* I thought. *I can't start crying when I see the first animal.*

"Let's all get into a circle," I told the group. "Pick a spot, and sit down. You don't have to push, Mike. There is plenty of room for everyone."

"And we need to be as quiet and calm as possible," Kathy said, pointing to the cages surrounding us. "These animals behave much better when they sense they are safe."

That's for sure, I thought sarcastically. I wished that all my animals were safe from flying rocks and the animal control people.

When the kids had settled down, Kathy brought out a snake, an opossum, a raccoon, and a very sleepy owl.

"Each of these animals has a story to tell about its life before it came to the museum. Many were captured and kept as pets, but their owner didn't know how to take care of them. Some are blind or missing a limb from being caught in a trap. So, although these animals seem tame when we're holding and petting them, they are still wild animals. That means that their instincts tell them to scratch or bite you if you anger them."

Kathy talked about the turtles that had nearly died, because people thought it was funny to spray paint on them. "Their shells couldn't breathe, so they were slowly suffocating," she said.

My thoughts turned to my turtles waiting for me at home. I wondered how they were doing. Before I left, I had put a screen top over the top of their tank. But would that be enough if a big rock landed on it? I felt the tears begin to well up in my eyes, and I blinked hard to keep them from flowing down my cheeks.

"Linda Jean," Mrs. Williams said, breaking into my thoughts. "Why don't you tell the children some of the stories about your animals?"

I looked at Mrs. Williams and then at the children's eager faces. No, I just couldn't do it. My eyes misted over, and I quickly excused myself to go to the bathroom.

When I pushed open the restroom door, I saw Krissy standing in front of the mirror. She was putting on the finishing touches to her clown's costume.

"You look awful," Krissy said when she saw my face.

"Well, I feel awful," I admitted. "Hearing all of Kathy's stories about abused animals makes me want to do something to save mine.

I can't think of anything else except my animals. I'm sorry."

I splashed cold water on my face, but it didn't help. "I feel like I'm going crazy," I said. "Did I tell you that I failed a Spanish test yesterday?"

"No, you didn't. That happened on top of the frog disaster with Mr. Servey?" Krissy asked with wide eyes. Something like that would never happen to Krissy, because she keeps a calendar with her life completely organized on it. She knows just when everything is due.

"I didn't have time to study last night because I was feeding all my animals. And the rock incident got me so worried that I couldn't even concentrate. I just wrote on my test that I was sorry and turned it in."

"This is getting worse than I thought," Krissy said. "I know you don't want to hear this, Linda Jean, but maybe you do have too many pets."

My eyes opened wide. "How dare you say that?" I asked her. "What would they do without me?"

Krissy finished applying her clown makeup and turned to look at me. "I'm not trying to make you angry. But think about it," she said calmly. "Your animals take up so much of your time. And this summer, your animals had babies. So, that's more responsibility for you than ever."

"But I take care of all of them as well as I can," I said defensively.

"What about when the babies grow up and need their own cages? What will you do then? Will you stack cages on top of cages?" Krissy asked.

"I don't know. I haven't thought about that yet," I admitted.

"What about the broken locks on two of your cages? Have you had a chance to fix them yet?"

"I haven't had time," I told her. "What is this, Krissy, the third degree?"

"No, I'm just being a good friend by showing that I care about your problem."

There was a knock on the door, and then Aimee walked in. "Are you two coming out?" Aimee called. "The kids are moving into the party room now."

"We'll be out in a minute," Krissy said. "I just have to put on my nose."

Aimee went back out to join the group, and

Krissy turned back to me. "All I'm saying is that you should think about all your animals. If you did give a few away, then you would have more time to spend with the rest of them."

"Okay, I'll think about it," I gave in. "But it's not easy for me to think about picking which ones to keep and which ones to say good-bye to. I'm not promising anything, or agreeing with you, Krissy. But I will think about it. Okay?"

"Yes. That's fair enough," Krissy said with a grin.

Five

I knew Krissy was just trying to help me by suggesting that I give away some of my pets. I did think about her idea—a lot. I thought about it on the way home from the museum, and as I changed clothes to take Mascot for a walk.

I knew Krissy was right, though. My pets did take up too much of my time. But thinking about giving away some of my animals and really doing it were two very different things. I loved them all so much—too much to pick the ones I would say good-bye to.

Mascot sniffed at a geranium bush. The red flowers tickled his nose, and he sneezed.

As we walked down the street, I could see that Mrs. Marlowe was in her yard trimming the branches on her trees. I looked the other way as we walked by. We went around the corner and down to the end of the next street. There was a vacant lot there that Mascot and I played in during the summer.

As we stood in the field, I realized that I would have to face Mrs. Marlowe sooner or later. If she was the one who had complained about my animals, then talking with her could solve the problem. *If I was really nice to Mrs. Marlowe, maybe I could get her to drop her complaint,* I thought. But I couldn't imagine her throwing rocks into my backyard.

During the walk home, I decided to go talk to Mrs. Marlowe. I took a deep breath and headed for her yard. She was carefully snipping the scraggly tips off the English Laurel hedge that lined her walkway.

"Mrs. Marlowe?" I called out to her.

She turned around to look at me. Her lips pressed into a straight line. "Yes?" she asked sternly.

"Mrs. Marlowe, I just wanted to apologize for Saucy, my pet skunk. He didn't mean any harm to your garden the other day. He got loose from his cage, and we were trying to catch him."

Mrs. Marlowe just looked at me and didn't

say anthing, so I kept on talking.

"My friends and I are sorry about trampling through your yard. I know that most people don't like skunks the way that I do."

I shut my mouth before I said too much and made her even more angry. She kept looking at me and didn't talk.

"Anyway, I wanted to stop to tell you that." I started to walk off, but Mrs. Marlowe called after me.

"You're right," she said to my back. "Skunks do have a stinky reputation."

When I turned around to look at her, I couldn't believe what I saw. Mrs. Marlowe actually was smiling at me. I wasn't sure whether she was trying to be funny or not, so I didn't laugh.

"Yes, they sure do," I finally said. "But I can't imagine why they do."

"Oh, I can," Mrs. Marlowe said, walking toward me and pulling off her rubber gardening gloves. "When I was about 10 years old, a skunk sprayed me in the apple orchard behind my parents' farm. When I think back to that time, I can still remember that terrible smell and how it wouldn't go away. I had to take at least 10 baths and bury my favorite shirt in the backyard. I wasn't very happy about that."

"So, Saucy brought back those awful memories for you?" I prompted, realizing that was why she had been so angry.

"No, that wasn't it. Saucy wrecked my herb garden," Mrs. Marlowe said. She pointed to a bare patch where her herb garden used to be. "I had been babying those sage plants since last fall. But you and your skunk fixed all that for me. Now I have to start all over again. It's very frustrating."

"Oh, Mrs. Marlowe, I'm really very sorry. My friends and I were so busy trying to catch Saucy that we didn't look where we were going," I said. "I'm really very responsible with my animals, and I spend a lot of time taking special care of each of them. I would never just let Saucy run loose to cause problems for anyone."

"Oh, I know that. I'm not angry anymore. I was able to save clippings of most of the plants, and I'm rerooting them indoors." Mrs. Marlowe's eyes looked softer now, and she didn't look so mean to me.

"So, you didn't report me to the Animal Control people?" I blurted out.

"Heavens no. Why would I want to do that?

I'm a pet lover myself," she said.

"You have pets?" I asked her.

She shook her head. "No, I don't now. But I used to have a parakeet and a cat. They were very special to me and great company to have around the house. When they died, I didn't have the heart to replace them."

"I know just how you feel," I said sympathetically.

Mrs. Marlowe was easy to talk to. Before I knew it, I had told her about the complaint, and my fears that I would have to give my animals away. I took Mascot home, and then I went back to help Mrs. Marlowe fix up her yard.

"You know, it has been kind of lonely since Mindy, my kitty, died. I've kind of replaced the attention I gave them with time in my garden," Mrs. Marlowe said.

"Well, I've really enjoyed this afternoon," I said truthfully. "But I'd better go home now. I know that my dad wants me to be on time for dinner."

"Stop by again, Linda Jean. But don't feel that you have to bring Saucy," she teased.

"Don't worry. Saucy prefers life in my backyard," I replied.

Feeling great, I jogged down the street and around the corner of the house. After talking all afternoon about my animals, I couldn't wait to see them. But my happy mood vanished when I saw the backyard. Rocks and wads of paper littered the yard and the patio where I kept the cages. I could have kicked myself for not being there when it happened.

"At least we know it isn't Mrs. Marlowe," I told the animals, who were quiet but scared. Regina hid in the corner of her cage with her babies cuddled beneath her. "There's no way that she could've thrown rocks and talked to me at the same time."

"Hey, Linda Jean," Joy called over the gate. "Are you back there?"

"Come on back," I said. "The rock thrower has struck again."

"Oh, no," Joy said as she looked around the yard. "Boy, what a mess."

"I'm happy that none of my animals were hurt this time," I admitted. "It's a good thing that I secured the screen top on the turtle tank. Look at this." I picked three rocks off the screen and pointed to the dents that the rocks had made.

"What does this person have against

turtles?" I wondered aloud.

But Joy wasn't paying any attention to me. She was staring at the huge oak tree that hung over into our backyard from the neighbors' yard that was directly behind us.

"Do you think that someone could be climbing that tree and throwing the rocks into your yard?" Joy asked.

"No way," I said. "The Murphys live behind us. And they're both very old and sick. They have a nurse who comes in to help them take baths and stuff. I don't think they are capable of climbing trees."

"Okay, it was just an idea," Joy said. "But that tree is the perfect way for someone to toss rocks into your turtle tank. Do you know the neighbors who live on either side of the Murphys?"

"No, I don't. I know one of those homes was sold recently. And I've never paid any attention to the other home," I said.

"We should take a walk over there on the way home from school Monday. We might find some kind of clue," Joy suggested.

I thought about her idea for a moment. "Well, we've already considered everyone on Honeybee Court and ruled them out. So, I guess you're right. We'll move on over to the next street and start finding out who lives there. But I know for sure that it's not the Murphys."

We piled up the rocks near the fence and threw the paper wads into the trash. I dragged a few sheets of plywood out of the garage and braced them against the posts on the patio.

"I'm not going to be scared into giving up my pets," I told Joy. "This will protect them until I can find out who is doing this. Then I'm going to report *them*."

We placed bricks against the bottom of the wood to keep the wind from knocking the shelter over. Then we stood back to admire our handiwork.

"They won't get as much light this way," I pointed out. "But it's better than letting them be hurt by flying rocks."

Joy reached in and petted Lucy. "That's for sure. Hey, didn't I see you talking to Mrs. Marlowe this afternoon?"

"Yeah. With all this mess, I forgot to tell you about it. I went over to tell her I was sorry about Saucy and about messing up her garden. But she wasn't upset about it anymore. In fact, I'm sure that she didn't complain to the Animal Control people. I know it's Sunday, but do you think we could call a special Forever Friends Club meeting to talk about her? I have a few ideas."

It didn't take much of an excuse to get us all together. Joy called Krissy, and I called Aimee. They both got to my house in less than 10 minutes.

"Sorry, I'm late," Aimee said as she breezed through the front door. "Graham called after you did. He says hi to everyone."

"Hi," we all said back.

"Hi," Dad said as he walked into the living room.

We all burst into giggles.

"We were talking to Graham," I explained.

Dad looked around the room. "Where is he?"

"He's not here," I said.

"Oh, I see. Well, actually, I don't see. But I guess that doesn't matter," he said. "What are you girls doing?"

"I called an emergency meeting to talk about my animals. Dad, did you see anything strange out back today? I found more rocks in the yard when I got home this afternoon."

"No, I didn't, honey," he told me. "I was in

my office listening to tapes of some meetings. So, I wouldn't have heard very much going on out back," Dad said.

"This time there were paper wads along with the rocks," Joy spoke up.

"This is getting serious," Dad said. "I'm going to call Jill Sinclair right now and tell her what is happening."

"Would you hold off for a little while, Mr. Jacobs?" Joy asked. "Before you call her, Linda Jean and I have talked about checking out Camellia Street for any clues. It's getting dark now, but we plan to walk home that way tomorrow after school. Let us see what we can find out first, okay?"

"All right. I'll give it one more day. Then I'm going to call," Dad said sternly.

Dad agreed that we could fix a snack even though dinner would be ready soon. We raided the refrigerator and finally decided to fix a big bowl of popcorn.

As we crunched, I filled Krissy and Aimee in on my conversation with Mrs. Marlowe. "See, she was just angry at us for trampling her herb garden. She really spends a lot of time taking care of her plants. She even invited me to come back some time to visit."

Krissy leaned so far back in the chair that it almost tipped over. She caught herself just in time and then laughed. "Is that why you called the special meeting, Linda Jean?" she asked. "You just wanted to tell us about Mrs. Marlowe?"

"That's part of it," I said. "But I also wanted to ask for your help. I admit that it was Saucy's fault that Mrs. Marlowe's herb garden got trampled. But would you let Party Time's funds buy her some new herbs to make up for those that were killed? I mean, we were on our way home from a party and everything."

Aimee spoke up first. "I think that would be okay," she said. "It was our fault, too. We ran through her yard just as much as you did. It's only fair that Party Time helps repair her garden. There is a nursery near the television studio. I'm working Tuesday, and I could check out the prices if you want."

We agreed and then made another batch of popcorn.

"There's one more thing," I said after I unstuck a big kernel from my tooth. "I've been thinking a lot about what Krissy said to me at the museum. She suggested that I consider giving away some of my pets, because they're taking up so much of my time."

Aimee and Joy stared at Krissy and me like we were crazy.

"Well, not all of them," I added quickly. "But Mrs. Marlowe said that she has been lonely since her cat and bird died, and that she hasn't gotten new ones since then. I thought I might give her one of mine."

"Oh, Linda Jean, that's a fantastic idea," Krissy said with a big smile.

Dad walked into the kitchen.

"So, you have a fantastic idea? I mean, don't feel you have to tell dear old Dad. I mean, I just live here." His eyes sparkled. He loved to tease us.

We all stumbled over each other's words trying to tell Dad about the Mrs. Marlowe plan.

"What do you think?" I asked after we had finished.

Dad took a handful of popcorn and munched for a minute before he answered. "I think you need to be careful not to offend Mrs. Marlowe by giving her too many presents that she hasn't asked for. Plants are one thing, but a pet is another."

"Hey, I have an idea!" Joy exclaimed. "Why don't we take the herbs down and offer to plant them for her? Then she can show us her garden, and we can get to know her better. Afterward, we could invite her over to your house to see your pets."

I liked that idea. "So, when she's looking at the animals, we can pay attention to which one she might like," I added. "Then I'll give her the animal."

"I don't know what you needed my advice for," Dad said with a grin. "I guess I'll be getting back to my tape recorder now."

"Uh, Dad?"

"Yes?"

"Have you thought about dinner?" I asked him sweetly. "You know that popcorn isn't very filling."

He looked at the clock on the wall. "I guess it is getting to be that time. How about if we all go out for hamburgers?"

A loud "Yes" rang through the room.

Six

"IT'S been a week, and we still haven't solved the rock mystery," I said with a big sigh. "I still don't know who is trying to make me get rid of my pets."

Krissy, Aimee, Joy, and I were skating around on the ice in the Atlanta Skating Emporium while we waited for Graham to arrive. He was going to help us with Susan Kopolas' skating party.

"I don't know what more we can do," Krissy said. "We walked down Camellia Street every day after school this week, but we never saw anyone outside. The only thing left is to go door to door and ask to talk with the people."

I sighed. "Yeah, that's an idea. It's too bad that we have to be at the party today."

"What do you mean?" Joy asked. "I thought

we all loved to skate."

"I didn't mean that, Joy. Most of the rock throwing happens during the day while we're at school or putting on parties. I just wish that I could be there today to try to catch the culprit."

"Well, today's Sunday. A lot of people do things and go places on Sunday. So, maybe nothing will happen today," Aimee said sensibly. "There's Graham." She spotted him first as usual.

We skated around the rink twice while Graham laced up his skates. Joy did a few leaps and twirls. It seems like nothing stops that girl from doing some dancing.

"Any more luck on the pet problem?" Graham asked after he had skated out to where we stood in the center of the rink.

We all shook our heads.

He skated a circle around me. "You know, Linda Jean. I still haven't told you about my idea. I know a place where you could take your pets. And I'm positive that the people would be absolutely thrilled."

"Hey," I said. "Let's forget about my pets for the rest of the party, okay? I get a headache every time I start worrying about them.

And I would like to have some fun today."

"Okay," Graham said. "But just remember that I'm here if you want to hear about it."

Saying my decision to stop worrying aloud put me in a good mood for the party. Susan Kopolas and her friends began arriving, and Graham headed to the booth to talk to his friend, Nick. We had met Nick briefly last week when we came to practice our skating before the party.

Joy and I went to the door to greet the kids. We gave them name tags and colored sashes to wear on their arms. The rink schedules several party sessions at one time, so we wanted to be able to spot Susan's friends easily. The arm sashes would help us keep track of everyone.

"Here's the plan," I said to the 10 kids who sat in front of me. Most of them were about seven or eight years old. "We'll all skate for about an hour. Then we'll play some games on the rink. Graham's friend Nick is the owner's son, so Nick and Graham will be our announcers today."

"Yeah!" the group shouted together. *Little kids are great*, I thought. They are full of excitement about everything. They don't worry about being cool. Kids that are Susan's age just shout and have a great time. They don't care if anyone is watching. I think that's why we all like putting on parties so much.

Nick started the music. A new tune that I liked blared out of the speakers. Nick announced that it was an "all skate."

I led the group out onto the rink. We kept our line together down the length of one wall. A few kids wanted to skate at their own pace. Joy took three of the better skaters to the center of the rink to show them some advanced moves. As we watched, Susan managed to spin around three times in one place without falling down, and Laura did a small leap.

The rink was beginning to fill up now with the other party groups. Krissy left to go put on her clown costume. She always waited until the party was underway to change, because she enjoyed surprising the kids.

The music finally stopped, and the big lights went on. It made the slick floor shine. Graham's voice came over the loudspeaker.

"Attention skaters. It's time to do the limbo!" The drumbeat song of the limbo filled the room, and kids lined up in the center of the rink. Graham and Nick brought out a pole.

"Will you be in charge of this?" Nick asked me. When he smiled, the lights glinted off his braces.

"Sure," I said, smiling back at him.

"He's cute," Aimee said to me as the boys skated back to the sound booth.

"Now, don't get any ideas, Aimee Lawrence. You already have Graham."

"I didn't mean for me. I meant for you," she said with a sly grin.

I knew that my face was turning pink. "Oh," I said. I found myself watching Nick instead of the kids who were waiting for Graham to demonstrate the limbo.

"Pay attention," Aimee whispered to me. "Here comes Graham."

"Do you think he saw me staring at him?" I asked.

"No, your staring was very subtle."

"I hope so," I said.

Graham skated past us. "Okay, kids. I'll show you how the limbo goes, and then you try to follow me," he announced. "Okay, put the pole halfway down like this."

"Yes, sir!" Aimee said.

"Please," he added with a grin. They both smiled at each other.

We lowered the pole, and Graham demonstrated for all of us. He definitely was entertaining. To do the limbo, the skaters must use their leg strength to arch their backs as low as the pole is. The skater must skate beneath the pole without touching it and without falling down.

Graham was strong. He did the dance while holding onto both knees. Then he went under the pole holding one leg while his other leg was extended out in front.

"Okay, try it those ways or any way you can to get under the pole without falling down," Graham said as he started to leave.

"Stay out here to limbo with us, Graham," Susan called. "I'll bet we beat you even with all your fancy moves."

"That's a challenge I can't ignore," Graham said, spinning around and heading for the end of the line near Susan. "Start the music, Nick. I'm ready to limbo."

The music filled the room again, and I did my best to pay attention to the game and not Nick. But every time I turned to help a child who had fallen, I caught him looking at me. Then he would flash one of his incredible smiles at me, and I would duck my head pretending not to notice.

"I think he likes you," Aimee said as we began a new game.

"No, he was just being friendly."

"People aren't friendly unless they like you," Aimee added. I could see that she wasn't going to stop talking about Nick.

Graham skated out and placed a large orange cone at one end of the rink. We stood with the kids at the other end of the rink.

"Okay, everyone," Nick said over the loud speaker. "You have to listen very carefully. Watch the clown, because she knows what she is doing."

I hadn't noticed that Krissy had come out onto the rink. Krissy the clown did a little twirl and bowed to the audience. She did a few skating moves and pretended to slip and fall. The kids giggled. "Okay, well, maybe she doesn't know what she's doing," Nick said.

Krissy picked herself up. I wished that I could skate as well as Krissy, Aimee, Graham, and Joy do. Joy is an especially graceful skater, and she even knows how to skate backward. I really wished I could do that, because that's what couples do when they skate together. I had tried plenty of times, but I couldn't get enough speed up.

Nick was great at red-light-green-light. He fooled the kids with just about any phrase he used. Sometimes he said, "green pickles" or "red lightning." If anyone moved, he spotted them and sent them back to the wall.

"Nick's funny, too," Aimee pointed out. Then she quickly excused herself to get the craft supplies ready.

"Quit pushing me," I said as she skated away.

"I think you should get to know him. That's all."

"Hey, do you need any help setting up the crafts?" I called to her.

"No, it's all organized," Aimee replied. Since the party was mainly skating, she had only planned a small craft.

Susan won the red-light-green-light game. It seemed like a different kid won each game. *How did Nick manage to do that?* I wondered. *It couldn't have been a coincidence.*

"Franklin party, your party room is now ready," Nick announced. "Stiles party, your room is also ready. Okay, one more song, and the Kopolas' party room will be ready. Would all of Susan Kopolas' friends please stay out on the rink until I call you?"

The lights dimmed, and the mirrored ball in the center of the rink turned and sprinkled specks of dancing light all over the floor.

"This is a couples skate," Nick announced. "Take a partner. You have to have a partner or exit the floor."

I was helping Susan and Marcy get into rhythm when I felt a tap on my shoulder. I turned around and looked into Nick's blue eyes.

"Do you need a partner?" Nick asked.

I was glad that the room was darkened, because I was sure that I blushed. I couldn't help it.

He took my hand. "Remember me from the other night? I'm Nick," he said. "And you're Linda Jean, right?"

"Right."

"I wanted to tell you that I'm sorry to hear about your pets. Graham mentioned it to me," he said, executing a neat turn and skating backward in front of me. He was still holding my hands.

"I'm sure it will all work out," I said. I wasn't sure, but what else could I say? I couldn't tell all my problems to a boy I didn't even know.

"Let's switch," he said, pulling me around in a circle and pushing me backward.

"Wait!" I shrieked. "Hold on. I don't know how to skate backward."

"What are you talking about? You're skating backward right now," Nick said with a grin.

I looked at my feet and then back up at Nick. I turned my head around to see where I was going.

"You don't have to do that. I'll look out in front of us. Your job is to make sure that no one slams into us from behind."

"I really can't skate backward," I said. My eyes flitted around the room. There wasn't any place to look, but at him. "I'm only going backward because you're pushing me."

"Okay, then. Do you want a lesson? I've been skating all my life, because my parents own the rink. I'd be glad to give you a few pointers."

"Don't you have to be back at the booth to announce?" I asked.

"Not until the song is almost over. But if you don't want to skate with me, I'll leave," he said quickly.

Nick had stylish bangs that swooped down and back up on the side and tiny curls peeking out behind his ears. He was even cuter when he smiled. I realized that the frown meant he was waiting for my answer.

"I'd like a lesson, really," I said.

It only took Nick a second to tell me what I was doing wrong. We stopped on the side corner, and he showed me how to start skating backward from a stopped position. It was easy once he told me to bend and straighten my knees and push my toes in and out.

Then he took my hands and we skated once more around the rink before the song ended. This time I knew I was helping to push us, because we practically flew past the other skaters. It was great. I had never felt so comfortable on skates before.

We stopped near the exit closest to the party rooms.

"I hope you'll come back again, Linda Jean. You're really very good. We give skate-dancing lessons here on Sunday mornings, too."

Nick skated back to the booth before I had a chance to answer, or to tell him I was always busy on Sunday mornings taking care of my pets.

He flipped on the rink's lights and called for the Kopolas party. There was no more time to think about Nick or the excitement I felt after skate-dancing. Susan and her guests took up the rest of the afternoon.

While we were cleaning up, Graham came over to work near me.

"You two looked like professionals out there," he said. "Have you ever thought of taking lessons?"

"No, I'm too busy with school, Party Time, and my animals. But it was fun."

"Speaking of animals," Graham began again, "I've been trying for a week to tell you about Orchid Gardens Retirement Center."

I took a deep calming breath and let it out. "Okay, I know you aren't going to let this rest until I let you talk, so spit it out," I told him.

"Nick's grandmother lives at Orchid Gardens," he said, ignoring the tone in my voice. "He goes to visit her there all the time, and I've gone twice. They have a special program there for the residents. It's called Pets for Seniors. The retirement complex has discovered that the health of senior citizens actually improves when they have a pet for company. My mom even produced a *Weekend Mag* special about the program."

"So, what does that have to do with me?"

I asked him glancing around the rink.

"They need more pets. The program has been so successful that more of the residents are asking for animals. The animal shelter has plenty of dogs and cats to offer, but many of the people at the home cannot get around to walk a dog or to chase after a cat. That's where your animals come in."

"I suppose you're saying that a bird or a turtle might be more appropriate," I said.

"Well, all I'm asking is that you think about it, Linda Jean," Graham said.

"I'm sorry, Graham. I know that you're just trying to help, but I haven't had any more complaints about my pets. And I won't consider doing anything else until I have to. They mean too much to me."

"I know that. But what if you do have to give them up?"

"If I do, and that's a very big if, Graham," I said, "I will definitely know who to call. So, let's drop it for now."

Seven

MY determined mood lasted only until I reached the front door to my house. Taped to the center of the door was a large note that read: *Your pets are noisy and smelly and a threat to the health of the neighborhood. If you don't get rid of them, I will call the police.*

My hands shook, making me drop the note. "Dad!" I yelled. "Dad!"

He opened the door in a hurry. "What happened? What's wrong?"

I bent down and picked up the note. "Look at this. Did you hear anything or see anyone who would've put this on our door?"

He took the note from me and scanned it quickly. "I'm sorry, honey. But I didn't." Dad put his arm around me and helped me inside.

I was shaking so hard that I knew I would fall if I didn't sit down.

"Sit here," he said, guiding me over to the living room couch. "I'm going to call the police myself. These threats have got to stop."

I listened to Dad's angry voice on the phone and tried to calm myself down. *Why was someone doing this to us? Who was trying to hurt my pets by throwing rocks into our backyard?* I felt so helpless.

My fears only grew when Dad hung up the phone and shook his head. "The police made me call Animal Control. Ms. Sinclair says there is nothing we can do unless we actually see the person who is harassing us."

"We can have a constant stakeout for the front door, but I doubt they'd put another note up. Would they, Dad?" I asked.

"I doubt it, too. But we should watch the backyard closely and make sure your animals are okay. Maybe we should move a few of them indoors tonight just in case any more rocks are thrown."

Getting all of the animals situated for the night took a while. Afterward, I was exhausted and went to bed early. But instead of a rock storm, there was a huge thunderstorm. As soon as I heard the first roar of thunder, I jumped out of bed and knocked on Dad's door just as Mascot began to howl.

"We have to stop meeting like this," Dad said in an attempt at a joke as we stumbled down the stairs together.

I didn't say anything. I just keep moving. Rain splattered on the plastic that I'd placed over the cage area. The rain began softly and then picked up until it was an incredible downpour. It sounded like 400 tap dancers were pounding on the thin plastic.

"This is the worst thing that could happen," I said, looking around at the animals. "They get so worked up in a storm."

As if on cue, Mascot began howling. Mandy joined him with a yowl loud enough to wake the neighbors. Dad quieted one, and I soothed the other. But it was not enough. Every crack of lightning sent the animals into a wild, screeching, howling frenzy.

This has to stop, I thought. *I can't go on like this much longer.*

The next morning as I dragged myself out of bed, I thought about the night before. I had spent hours trying to keep the animals quiet. I had feared for their safety. But suddenly, in the middle of all the chaos, I realized that I wasn't managing very well. Even though Dad had helped, we were only able to comfort one or two animals at a time. The other 17 had to fend for themselves.

It was impossible to keep my eyes open in school that day. The week of worrying had finally taken its toll on me. During Mrs. Wright's class, I tried to pretend that I was working. She gave us a writing assignment, so I put my pencil on my paper and propped my forehead in my hand.

I closed my eyes and tried to look like I was working. But my head kept falling off of my hand. I'd jerk it up, open my eyes, and try to focus on Mrs. Wright and what she was writing on the blackboard. But before long, my eyelids would get heavy, and I'd be dozing again.

I jerked up my head as the class bell rang. "Turn your papers in as you leave class," Mrs. Wright said.

I looked at the paper in front of me. There were a few real words and a bunch of scribbles where my hand had continued to write as I fell asleep. I slipped the paper into my notebook and tried to sneak out of class without

Mrs. Wright seeing me. I was hoping to do the assignment during lunch and sneak back into my English class to put the paper in the stack.

"Miss Jacobs, will you stay after class for a moment?" Mrs. Wright asked.

I was caught.

I waited until the rest of the class had filed out of the room. Joy gave me a sympathetic look. "I'll wait outside," she whispered to me.

"It's okay," I said honestly. "I don't want you to miss your next class. I'll see you at lunch."

"I hope Joy isn't waiting for you," Mrs. Wright said as soon as we were alone. "This may take longer than the five minutes you have between classes. I'll give you a pass to get into your next class."

"I'm sorry that I fell asleep in class today," I told her, figuring that I might as well apologize up front.

"Falling asleep in class is only one of the problems that I understand you have had lately. Mrs. Garcia tells me that you failed a Spanish test, and Mr. Servey says you walked out on a frog dissection the other day. Even worse, he said you never showed up in study hall. I assume you left school, which you know is a big offense around here. I'm very surprised that Mr. Servey didn't turn you in."

"He's making me write an extra report and dissect the frog by computer," I explained to her.

"Have you completed today's assignment for this class?" she asked. I looked up, and Mrs. Wright was staring at me waiting for my answer.

"No, I didn't," I admitted.

"This isn't like you at all," she said.

I shuffled my feet, drawing circles with my toes on the floor in front of me. "I've had a lot on my mind lately."

But Mrs. Wright wouldn't accept my vague explanation. "Is there some kind of trouble at home, Linda Jean?"

She sat down next to me and pointed to a seat beside her. "I don't want you to think that I'm angry at you or disappointed in you. But I wouldn't be a good teacher if I didn't notice when one of my students has problems outside of class. You've always been a very good student, Linda Jean. I'm concerned about this change in your work habits."

Her eyes were kind as she sat there patiently waiting for me to talk about my problems.

I remained silent.

Mrs. Wright was one of my favorite teachers, but I didn't feel like discussing my personal troubles with her. I was scared that I would break down and cry in front of her. Then she would really think that I was a mess. I also was worried that she would agree with Krissy and the complainer—that I should find other homes for my pets.

"I don't feel like talking about it," I told her. "I guess I need to find my own solutions to my problems."

"That's fair enough," Mrs. Wright said, getting up and walking behind her desk. "But until you solve your problems on your own, I'm going to assign you to after-school detention. The time you'll spend there should be enough to catch up on your homework."

"Detention?" I shrieked. "I have too many things to do at home." *And, besides, I'd never gotten into trouble at school in my whole life,* I wanted to cry out.

"You also have assignments for school. I'm not giving you detention as just a punishment, Linda Jean. I think it'll give you the time that you need to catch up. It'll be some uninterrupted time to complete your assignments.

And that'll be one area where you'll have less stress. I'll even tell the detention teacher that you may leave early if you finish early. Okay?"

"I guess I should say thank you," I said, trying to smile.

"No thanks are necessary," she said.

"Then I won't say it," I mumbled to myself as I walked toward the door holding the pass that she had written for me.

"That's the spirit!" Mrs. Wright called after me. "Maybe being angry at me will motivate you to do your homework."

I walked as fast as I could down the hall. I was so embarrassed. *How could she have heard me?* I wondered. I was careful not to run in the hall though, or I'd be breaking another school rule. But what did it matter really if I did? I already had detention. The word made my stomach queasy and a lump form in my throat. Detention was given to jerks. Why was this happening to me?

Things got even worse when I realized that detention meant I would miss part of our Forever Friends Club meetings after school. When I told my friends the news at lunch, they were pretty sympathetic about it. Even Aimee was understanding. I thought she might be especially angry because I had given her a difficult time when she missed meetings to help Graham learn to read.

But even talking to my friends didn't make me feel any better.

After school, I went to the study hall room for detention. I looked around at the six other kids who sat spread out around the room. I tried to concentrate on my homework. I just had to finish the English assignment that I had slept through and study for the make-up Spanish test. And I still had to find time to dissect that frog on computer and then write a big report on it.

Even with all my school problems, my mind kept drifting to home and my animals. *Were Oswald and Percival okay? Had more rocks been thrown today? Will another note be taped to the front door when I get home?*

Lately, my pets were taking up all of my spare time and all of my thoughts. I was beginning to wonder whether I should listen to Graham's idea. I mean, if I didn't have to worry so much about rocks and complaining neighbors, I could think about fun things like Nick and skating. I really wanted to take skating lessons, but when did I have the time? And now I even had detention every day.

I folded my unfinished papers and put them in my backpack. The big black hands on the clock announced that time was up. I stood up and followed the others out of the room.

With my head bent against the wind, I didn't even see the red convertible waiting for me near the curb. I heard the horn honk, though. There were three long blasts and then an "ooogah" sound.

"Mom!" I shouted, running down the steps to meet her. "How did you know I'd be here?"

"I was there when you called your dad at work to tell him about detention. He said you might need some cheering up, so here I am!"

"I notice the top is up," I said as I buckled my seatbelt. "I guess you don't play Lewis' up or down game with the car rooftop in the winter." Lewis is my stepdad.

"No, during the winter when Lewis asks us which we prefer, we just stick our tongues out and shiver," Mom said with a big grin. "So, what's new with you?" She pulled out into the traffic on Grove Street. "Your dad told me about your problem with the animals."

I really didn't feel like talking about it again, so I changed the subject. "Mom, do you miss

California much?" I asked. "How are Josh and Stephanie doing with the build-it-yourself airport I gave them for Christmas? Have they lost all the pieces yet?"

Mom gave me a knowing look that I had avoided her topic. "They have already put it together, taken it apart, and turned it into a space station and a farm."

"I knew it would be a good gift," I said.

She stopped at the light on Grove Street and drove down Mason Avenue to the shopping mall. She pulled into a parking space and turned off the engine.

"Okay, Linda Jean. You have a choice. Do you want to tell me what is bothering you, or do you want to shop?" she asked.

My mom is great. She knows when to let me talk and when to give me space. Since she and her new family moved to Atlanta, the two of us get together a lot to have fun and to get to know each other again.

"I want to shop!" I shouted.

"Well, let's do it!" Mom said with a smile.

We ran from the car to the mall entrance. It was hard pulling the doors open against the wind. Once we got inside, we took a second to smooth our hair back in place.

"Okay, where to?" I asked.

"How about Fashion Express? I hear they're having a great sale on sweaters. If today's weather keeps up, it looks like we're going to need some."

"I could use some of those stretchy black pants. I'm thinking about taking some skate-dancing lessons."

"Skate-dancing?" Mom asked. "Don't you need a partner for that?"

"Maybe there will be someone in my class," I answered mysteriously as I saw the knowing look in her eye. "Well, there is this one guy named Nick who I skated with at Susan's party."

"And?" she prompted.

"And Nick's family owns the Atlanta Skating Emporium. So, he's been skating all his life."

"And?" Mom asked again.

Okay, so I gave up trying to act cool. I spun around in front of the mirror, letting the sweater I'd tried on spin with me. "It was so much fun, Mom. He skated with me and taught me to skate backward. I felt like I was flying."

"You better watch it," she whispered. "The

85

sales clerk thinks you're going to do something to that sweater."

"Oh, I'm sorry," I said, smiling at the clerk.

Mom and I giggled as we went back into the dressing rooms.

"Nick sounds like a nice boy," Mom said as she changed clothes.

"I don't know him very well," I told her. "But he has a nice smile, and he's very friendly. He even told me that I was a good skater."

"How do you like this one?" Mom asked, pushing her door open.

"It's too baggy," I said. "What do you think of my sweater?"

"It's too tight and too green," she replied after studying it for a minute.

"What about the pants?" I held up the sweater so she could see how the waist fit.

"Turn around," Mom instructed.

I did.

"They look very nice, honey. They fit you well, and they look comfortable enough to skate in." She looked at me with a knowing grin.

"Yeah, I think they're good, too," I said.

There are some things that you just can't discuss with your friends or with your Dad, I thought. I watched Mom pay for the pants. I realized how happy I was that she lived in Atlanta now, and that we could spend special mother and daughter times together.

We stopped at a few more stores. Mom bought a purple zippered jacket. We lingered at the jewelry counter and finally selected a wild pair of earrings from the sale table.

"No one would know you're my mother," I told her honestly. "You're so much fun sometimes." I didn't have to explain what I meant. I knew she understood.

"Thanks, honey. I wanted to cheer you up," Mom said.

"You have," I told her, giving her a hug. "You have!"

Eight

DURING the drive home from the mall, I began getting that weird, uneasy feeling that you get sometimes when something is wrong or when someone is staring at you. Twice I turned around and looked out the back window to see if another car was following us. But no one unusual was there.

But the queasy feeling grew as we rounded the corner onto Honeybee Court. The dark imprint of recent tire tracks onto the driveway was the first thing I noticed when we neared our house. The tracks were different than the ones my Dad's car makes.

"Thanks, Mom. Shopping was fun."

"Call me if you want to talk," she said, giving me a big hug. "And Linda Jean, when this pet business is solved, Lewis and I would like to take you on a weekend vacation someplace fun."

"That would be terrific. I would like to spend some more time with you," I admitted. She waved, and I watched her car until it was out of sight. I really did miss Stephanie and Josh and Lewis, but I didn't have time to think about them. I jumped over the tire tracks and rushed to the door.

What could be wrong now? Please don't let it be another complaint, I thought.

I dropped my stuff in the entryway and followed the smells into the kitchen. "Was she here again, Dad?" I asked hurriedly. "Was Jill Sinclair here about my animals?"

One look at his face, and I knew. I slumped into a chair by the kitchen table and dropped my shopping bags onto the floor.

"I'm sorry," he said. "She brought the formal notice this time. It's there on the table if you want to read it."

I looked at the folded piece of official stationery and shook my head. The animal shelter stamp in the corner of the envelope did nothing to take away the pressured feeling that someone was trying to break my heart.

"I don't want to read it," I said. "Just tell

me what it says."

Dad stirred the spaghetti sauce and dropped the noodles into the pot of boiling water. "It says that you have 30 days to find other arrangements for your pets, or the county will come and take them away."

"Not that, Dad!" I yelled. "I can't bear that! Can we move away from here? Please?" I stood up and slammed my hands down on the table. "I won't let them take my pets! They'll kill them!"

"I know how you feel, honey. I feel the same way about this, but we can't move away. You know that."

"What are we going to do then?" I asked.

"I guess this is one time when we can't wait around to see what happens," Dad said. "We'll call a lawyer. At least if we fight this in court, we'll meet the person who is complaining face to face. Besides, we have a case of our own," he added, jabbing at the spaghetti noodles. "The animals wouldn't be making nearly as much noise if this person stopped throwing rocks at them."

The doorbell rang as I was about to agree. *How dare this person throw rocks and then complain about all the noise?* I thought as I went to answer the door.

Three voices hit me the minute I opened the door.

"What happened?" Joy asked. "We saw that Animal Control woman's car pull up in your driveway."

"Was detention as bad as everyone says?" Krissy asked.

"Boy, you look terrible," Aimee observed. "What can we do to help you?"

"Come on in," I said, overwhelmed by the questions and their support. "I'll tell you about everything. Just come inside."

Dad was setting our plates on the table when we entered the kitchen. "Have you all eaten?" he asked.

"No, we came right over to find out what was happening," Aimee spoke up. "Are we invited to stay?"

Dad grinned. "Of course, you are."

While Aimee and Krissy were calling their parents to tell them they'd be staying for dinner, Joy sat down next to me. "I don't have to call because Abby is catering another garden club meeting. We missed you at the Forever Friends Club meeting, Linda Jean," she said. "We got a call today from a new family on

Camellia Street. They heard about us from the Williams family, and they want us to do a birthday party for their seven-year-old son this coming weekend."

"That's great," I said unenthusiastically.

"That woman from the Animal Control brought bad news, huh?"

"Ms. Sinclair brought a notice that says I have to get rid of my pets." I burst into tears and grabbed a napkin to hide my face. I couldn't help it. Just thinking about living without my animals made me sick.

"We can't let them do this," Krissy said as she held onto me tightly. "There has to be a way to fight this."

"Dad said he would call a lawyer," I said. "But I don't know if we have time to fight it. The notice said only 30 days."

"Can't a lawyer get you some more time?" Joy asked.

"I don't know. Maybe I *should* give some of my pets away. Graham told me about a nice place where they could go."

"Are you crazy?" Aimee shouted. "You can't let them get away with this. You have to fight for your rights!"

Throughout dinner, I listened to my friends

come up with one scheme after another to save my animals. They talked about court battles, petition drives, and daytime watches. I was so tired of worrying and thinking about my pets, and of trying to live my life around their feeding schedules.

I listened quietly through dinner. Everyone assumed that I agreed with their Operation Animal Rights plan. I might have nodded my head when Aimee suggested having the neighbors sign a petition in favor of my keeping my animals. I think I agreed to talk to the people who refused to sign the petition. I'm not sure, though. I was so tired.

The last thing I remember is lying on the couch listening to Dad and my friends talking about my animals. I woke up as Dad was carrying me to bed.

I woke up early the next morning. The sun wasn't even close to rising, but I got up, anyway. I checked my sleeping pets and settled down with a cup of cocoa and a muffin at the kitchen table. I finished all my homework before it was time for school. I even finished some of that night's homework.

Just before Mrs. Wright's class, I went in and showed her how much work I'd done that morning. She said that if I did all my homework that night, she would lift my detention. She said she knew I was under stress at home, and that she didn't want to add to it by keeping me late every day.

I promised that once detention was over, I wouldn't let my schoolwork slide again. I almost flew out of science class to meet my Forever Friends on the schools steps.

"That was the shortest detention in history. How did you get out so fast?" Joy asked.

"Mrs. Wright said that I only had to go to detention until I caught up on my schoolwork. Well, I'm caught up now. Today I took the Spanish test over, and I even read a chapter ahead in English."

Krissy propped her book bag onto her shoulder. "When did you have time to do all this? You were zonked when we left last night."

"I woke up really early and finished it when I felt fresh this morning," I told her.

"So, there weren't any rock problems last night?" Aimee asked.

"No, thank goodness. They usually happen during the day when no one is home. I just wish I could figure out who's doing it," I said. "Are you sure it isn't the people right behind you?" Joy asked again.

"No. I keep telling you that they are both very old. The most exercise they get is reading," I stated sternly. "I don't think pitching rocks over the fence is their hobby. Anyway, I want to talk about something more cheerful."

"Okay, let's talk about taking the herb plants to give to Mrs. Marlowe," Aimee said. "I picked up the plants at the nursery, but we still haven't taken them to her. How about today?"

It sounded like a great idea, so we went to Joy's house first to grab a snack of Abby's leftovers from the garden club meeting. Then we went to Aimee's to gather up the plants. Together, we all trooped down the street to Mrs. Marlowe's house. She opened her front door before we even reached her porch.

"I was sitting by the front window," she explained. "I like to watch the street to see who is coming and who is going."

"We brought you some replacement herb plants," I told her. "Surprise!" We all took the plastic containers from behind our backs.

"How nice," Mrs. Marlowe said. She bent to smell the fragrant greenery. "Sage, Thyme,

Marjoram, and Rosemary. What a nice gift. Please come in."

I could tell that Aimee, Joy, and Krissy were surprised that she could be so nice after the skunk incident.

"It's our fault that your plants were destroyed in the first place," I said. "So, it's only right that we give you new ones. Would you like us to plant them for you?"

"That would be nice," Mrs. Marlowe said. "I'll get the tools and help you."

It only took us a few minutes to set the plants into the soil of her herb garden.

"These are healthy plants," she commented. "They'll be able to stand a frost or two before spring."

We brushed the dirt off our clothes and were getting ready to leave when she stopped us.

"You aren't going to leave yet, are you? I was hoping that you'd join me for some iced tea and a tour of my gardens in the back."

We couldn't turn her down. She had been so nice to us. Walking through Mrs. Marlowe's gardens was like taking a fantasy trip back in time. Stepping out of her back door was like stepping into the Victorian era.

"It's much prettier in the spring and summer," she said as if to apologize. "When the flowers are in bloom, it is truly a beautiful sight around here."

"Your garden is beautiful now," Joy said.

"Hey, you know what you need?" I asked her. "You need a parrot." The words slipped out before I even had the chance to stop them. My friends looked at me strangely.

"What I mean is, the colors of a parrot would stand out beautifully against the greenery in the garden. Any bird would."

Mrs. Marlowe's eyes had a far-away look to them. "I used to bring my parakeet out here in the summertime. He sang and sang, making the garden seem even more like paradise."

Then we all went inside for iced tea. All during our talk, I had the feeling that Mrs. Marlowe was the kind of person who could give good advice. When everyone decided it was time to go home, I stayed behind at Mrs. Marlowe's.

"Well, my friend, how has it been going with your animals? I worried about all of you during the thunderstorm the other night."

I took a sip of my iced tea and settled back on the padded cushions of her chair. "Actually, the situation with my animals isn't going so well. I received a notice yesterday that I have to find new homes for them in 30 days or turn them over to the county officials."

"That's awful!" Mrs. Marlowe exclaimed. "Well, I suppose you will fight this injustice in court, right?"

"That's what everyone else wants. My father has hired a lawyer. And my friends are making petitions to have the neighbors sign."

Mrs. Marlowe put down her cup, folded her hands, and looked directly at me. "And what do you want, Linda Jean?"

"You know I love my animals," I said quickly. "I don't want anything to happen to them. They are like my family."

She nodded, waiting for me to go on.

I took a deep breath and let it out slowly. I was doing a lot of that during the last two weeks. It helped me organize my thoughts.

"Lately my pets have been taking up too much time. I have to give each special attention, and then worry about whether they will start being noisy again. And then there are the rocks that someone keeps throwing into the yard and scaring the animals."

"Are there other things you want to do

besides baby-sit pets?" Mrs. Marlowe asked.

A quick image of Nick and the ice rink appeared in front of my eyes. "Yes," I told her. "There are things I want to do and things I have to do like schoolwork."

"Would you like more iced tea?" she asked, holding the pitcher above my glass.

"Yes, please."

"Then what are you going to do about your animals?"

It was a simple question, but the answer didn't come as easily.

I thought for a long moment. I had very mixed feelings. *What about my father who was helping by getting a lawyer for me? What about my friends who all jumped in to help me? Finally, I wondered, what about me?*

"If it was up to me alone," I began slowly, "I would take Graham's suggestion and give most of my pets away to the Pets for Seniors Program at Orchid Gardens. I might keep a few if the Animal Control people would let me, but I think I would give most of them to people there because they have the time to love them."

"Do you mean Orchid Gardens, the retirement complex?" she asked.

"That's the one," I said. "My friend Graham

knows someone who lives there. He says they are looking for some unusual pets for some of the residents."

"My sister lives there, too," Mrs. Marlowe said. Her eyes sparkled. "It's a wonderful place. And I think the people would be so excited. I know your pets would be very happy there."

"Do you really think so? I've been worried about them going to a sterile, hospital-type place," I admitted.

"Orchid Gardens isn't like that at all," Mrs. Marlowe explained. There's a big, beautiful lobby with lots of green plants. Each apartment has its own view of the landscaped yard area. There are year-round streams, fountains, walking trails, you name it. The people who live there walk their pets and visit with each other daily."

"I'd like to see it," I said finally.

"I know you'd have no trouble finding takers for your pets there. In fact," she said, the lines around her eyes crinkling into a smile, "I may even be interested myself. What kind of pets did you say you had?"

I grinned back at her. "I was just waiting for you to ask. But I can't possibly describe them all to you. You have to see for yourself."

Nine

"**L**OOK!" Krissy exclaimed. "I've gotten 17 signatures for the petition."

We were gathered in Joy's living room for our afternoon Forever Friends meeting. But instead of business, the talk kept shifting to the pet problem.

"So, who do we have left to talk with?" Aimee asked. "Did anyone refuse to sign?"

"No one refused," Joy said. "But there are a couple of houses we haven't gone to yet."

"What if the person who complained went ahead and signed the petition just to throw us off the track?" Krissy asked.

"I guess that's possible, but let's not give up until we've talked to the people at the last few houses," Aimee added. "Maybe we'll find the complainer yet."

I listened to my friends chatter about the petition and their plan to save my animals. But I didn't say anything. My heart wasn't in it. I also wasn't thrilled about the appointment that Dad had made with the director of Animal Control.

Mr. Simmons, Dad's lawyer, had come to our house for three hours the night before. We'd talked about every aspect of the problem.

Krissy, Aimee, and Joy were planning to come along to court as character witnesses (to say that I'm a good person) and to bring the petition.

How was I going to tell them that I had changed my mind?

I felt like a traitor. Everyone was working so hard to help me and my pets. And here I was deciding to give them away.

I did have one nice thing to think about. Mrs. Marlowe liked Percival the parrot so much that she took him home to live with her. I knew I would be able to visit him any time I wanted to, which made it easier. I also knew that he would have a loving home.

"Are we ready for the party on Saturday? How about you, Linda Jean?" Aimee asked.

"Huh? I guess I wasn't listening," I said.

"We're talking about the party for Ryan Eby, the seven year old who lives on the next street," she reminded me. "Boy, I can't wait until we get this pet problem solved. We need your full attention."

"You were all talking about the petition," I snapped. I took a deep breath and apologized again. After all, they didn't know that I was sick inside about telling them my decision.

We spent the next half hour planning the decorations and theme for Ryan's party. Since we'd picked a dinosaur theme, I decided to bring my turtles, my snake, and Lucy. Ryan's mother had said he liked reptiles, so it seemed perfect. And besides, Abby just loved grossing everyone out with her slime-green limeade punch.

"Where exactly does this Ryan kid live on Camellia Street?" I asked.

"His mom called to ask us about the party, but she didn't give us the address yet. She was in a hurry when she called from work. She said she would call us on Friday with the time, so we can get it then," Joy said.

"Nothing like waiting until the last minute," I told her.

"I figured it didn't matter," Joy remarked. "I mean, how hard can it be to find? They just live around the corner."

As I sat there thinking about which animals to take to the party, I suddenly thought that maybe the kids there would like to take home a turtle for a pet.

I hated to tell my friends what I was thinking about. They had all worked so hard to win my case. And I knew that I would be disappointing them and my dad.

As soon as I got home, I went to the phone and dialed Graham's number. "Hi, Graham," I said when he answered.

"Is that you, Linda Jean? I've been thinking about you."

"I've been thinking about you, too," I admitted. "I've been thinking about what you suggested the other day."

"Have you made any decisions?"

"Well, I talked to my friend, Mrs. Marlowe, who lives down the street from us," I said. "Her sister lives at Orchid Gardens, and she agrees that it's a nice place. She thinks my animals will be happy there."

"I hate to say I told you so."

"Go ahead," I said.

"I told you so," Graham said and then laughed.

"Well, I've been thinking about checking out that pet adoption program you talked about. Do you think you could go over there with me tomorrow?"

"Sure, I don't have to work at the studio."

"Do you mind if I bring Mrs. Marlowe along? She said she would like to come."

"I'll set it up with the director. And, Linda Jean, you won't be sorry," he added.

Later that night, I sat on my bed organizing all the photos that I had taken of my animals. I thought the photos would give the people at the home a good idea of what I was talking about. As I was finishing up, Graham called back to make sure that I hadn't changed my mind. We decided to go right after school before the Forever Friends Club meeting.

I was glad that Aimee would be working at the TV studio that day. It was one less chance of being found out before I was ready to tell them. I wrote Joy a vague note that I was walking home alone and put it in the handle of her locker.

I knew she would be curious, but I didn't want to try to explain or to lie. Mrs. Marlowe picked Graham and me up at school and drove us to the retirement complex.

"It's beautiful," I said as we drove into the tree-filled parking lot. The lobby was filled with plants and even a little waterfall. Residents sat comfortably in several living-room-type areas that were decorated with paintings and racks of magazines.

"We're here to see Mr. Rasmussen about the pet adoption program," Graham told the receptionist at the desk.

"He's expecting you. Go on in. His office is two doors down on the right," she said.

We went down the short hallway that she had pointed to and found the door to Mr. Rasmussen's office open. As I stood there, I began to panic. *Was I really doing the right thing by being here?*

But then Mr. Rasmussen greeted us, and my fears fell away. We told him our names.

"I'm very pleased to meet you," he said, shaking our hands. "Sit down. Make yourselves comfortable."

The walls of his office were covered with framed pictures of animals. Above the couch, there was a painting of two horses playing in a field of buttercups. Mr. Rasmussen picked up a sleepy cat next to him and put her on his lap.

"Graham says you have some unusual pets to donate to our adoption program," he said.

"Do you think anyone here would enjoy a squirrel family, a descented skunk, or an owl?" I asked. I told him about Gunther Goose, Regina Rabbit and her babies, and Taffy, Harry and Max, the turtles. I talked about every pet that I could remember and showed him the pictures that I'd taken.

"I know our residents will welcome your pets," he said, studying the pictures. Then he laughed. "This is a good one." He pointed to the picture I had taken of Lucy the Iguana carrying Max on her back. "Some residents may be a little frightened though, because they've only been exposed to dogs and cats."

"I could show my pictures to the people here and tell a little bit about each one," I offered.

Mrs. Marlowe spoke up. "I've seen Linda Jean's animal area. She takes excellent care of her pets. And I'm sure the adoptive parents would benefit from her information."

"Hey, I have a great idea," Graham said. "Why doesn't Party Time give a Pet Adoption party. Linda Jean, you could bring all your pets and show them to interested residents. You could give a little presentation on the needs of each. It's perfect."

Mr. Rasmussen smiled. "That's a brilliant idea, Graham. It would be a much faster way to distribute the pets. And it sounds like more fun than posting notices on the bulletin board. What do you say, Linda Jean?"

"I say, let's go for it. The sooner the better! I'll call you as soon as I set up a time with my friends." I felt better than I had in a long time. *But how was I going to break the news to my friends?*

That afternoon, I didn't have a single chance to tell them. We all split up during our meeting to shop for supplies for Ryan's party and to help Abby get the food ready.

Mrs. Eby finally called and told us the dimensions for her family room where the party was to be held. Krissy and Aimee rode off on their bikes to McLloyd's Discount Party store. Abby realized she was out of green sprinkles and eggs to make the cake, so Joy took off to the grocery store with a list.

I stayed to help Abby. She worked on making fresh noodles for a spaghetti fund raiser she was catering on Saturday night.

The Georgian School, a fancy private school, had liked her food so much the last time that they invited her back for their next event. They didn't need us to entertain the students this time because the dinner was the main event.

"How did we do these dinosaur sandwiches last time?" I asked. "Was it tuna and mustard inside or tuna and lettuce?"

"It was tuna and mustard," she answered. "We put the lettuce under the sandwich on the plate right before we served it."

I worked quickly. I set out 24 slices of wheat bread on the long counter. Then I spread mustard up one side and down the other. I followed with the tuna, then slapped the sandwiches together.

Dip, cut, cut, cut, dip. I dipped the dinosaur-shaped cookie cutter into water and then cut tyrannosaurus rexes out from the middle of each sandwich. We try to give the kids nutritious food that doesn't look like it's good for them. We disguise it as something fun.

Even when the others came back, I didn't tell them my decision. The timing just never felt right. We were so busy whipping up batches of gingerbread and salads that we worked mostly in silence.

Ten

WE decided to walk to Ryan Eby's party on Saturday. Abby was still working on munchies for her spaghetti dinner when we left from Joy's house. Everyone else's parents were busy for the day.

I gathered together Lucy, Harry, Max, and Barnaby, my snake. "I hope Ryan's house isn't too far," I said as we walked down Honeybee Court and turned the corner onto Camellia Street.

"Here's the address," Joy said. "It's 5640 Camellia."

"But that's the house right behind..." I began. But I didn't need to finish my thought because we were standing in front of 5640 Camellia Street. And we had just started walking. It was the house directly in back of mine—

the one with the big oak tree.

"I wonder what happened to the Murphys," I said.

"I thought they still lived here," said Aimee. "An older lady signed our petition the other day."

"Yeah, I never heard anything about their moving," Krissy added.

I rang the doorbell. "It's getting curiouser and curiouser," I said, quoting *Alice in Wonderland.*

"Welcome," Mrs. Eby said, greeting us at the door. "Ryan, come here," she called.

Ryan Eby was tall for a seven year old. *He was definitely tall enough to climb a tree,* I thought.

"How long have you been living here?" I asked him.

"For a while," he said proudly.

"We've been here about a month," Mrs. Eby said.

And that's when all the trouble started, I recalled.

"My mom's a nurse. She gives Gramps his medicine," Ryan told us.

The pieces of the puzzle were beginning to fall together. Ryan Eby and his mother had moved in with the Murphys to take care of them. I didn't want to jump to any wrong ideas, but I was certain that Ryan was the rock thrower.

I decided to wait until I had a chance to talk with him later about it. We set up for the party. Casually, I strolled into the backyard to check out the big oak tree. I found rocks along the flower bed near the fence—the same rocks that I had found in my backyard.

But there is no way that any boy could climb such a big tree, I decided. The first branch was about 10 feet off the ground. The only other way seemed to be throwing the rocks over the fence, but I didn't see how he could have enough strength to do that, either.

"It's still a mystery," I told Joy, Krissy, and Aimee as we set out the materials for the crafts project. "And I don't want to accuse Ryan unless I know for sure that he is the one that did it."

"You're being very calm about it," Joy said. "I'd be furious."

"Maybe he doesn't know any better," I defended him.

"He seems sweet enough," Aimee observed. "I can't imagine him trying to hurt your pets.

Look," she added, pointing to the kitchen counter, "Ryan and Lucy seem to be friends already."

Ryan was sitting on the counter stool with his nose pressed against Lucy's glass cage. Lucy was studying him just as closely.

The doorbell rang.

"Your friends are here, Ryan," I called to him. "Why don't you greet them with us at the door? You can help put the name tags on."

"Okay," he said brightly. He really was sweet. He had curly dark hair that flipped up on his collar in the back. His eyes were big and blue as he jumped around trying to do and watch everything at once.

"Do you like Lucy?" I asked as we walked to the door together.

"Uh-huh, and she likes me, too. We're friends."

"Lucy is a friendly iguana. Would you like to hold her later?" I asked him.

"Yes, please," Ryan said.

I smiled. "You have to promise to be careful though. Lucy is alive just like you and me. She is fragile."

"I'll be careful," he promised seriously.

All of Ryan's friends arrived within a few

minutes of each other.

"The first thing we are going to do is the treasure hunt," I told them, looking at their eager faces. "Everybody go out to the back-yard, and stand under the oak tree. I'll be out in a second with your first clue."

I sent Ryan and his friends into the yard. They were all so cute that I couldn't help smiling. But my laughter stopped when I stepped outside. Ryan and his six friends were pitching rocks over the fence. Most of the rocks didn't make it over the fence, but Ryan's did. He was using a slingshot.

His rocks were hitting their mark because I could hear Mac shrieking and Mascot bark-ing. The animal noises grew louder. The sounds of my animals' shrieks broke me out of my thoughts. "Stop!" I shouted at all of them. "You stop that this instant!"

Ryan turned toward me with his sling shot loaded to shoot. "Hi, Linda Jean," he said, with a big smile on his face. "Do you want to try?" He offered me his sling shot.

I told myself to calm down before I told him what I thought of his slingshot. "Ryan," I began slowly. "Do you know who lives on the other side of that fence?"

He shook his head. His smile was beginning to fade.

"I do," I told him. "I live on the other side of that fence, and so do all of my animals. Do you hear the noise going on over there—the barking and banging and screeching?"

He nodded. There was no smile left on his face.

"Some of your rocks have hit my pets. They are scared and hurt."

"I didn't mean to hurt them," he said.

The other kids dropped their rocks. I held my hand out for Ryan's slingshot.

"I know you didn't mean to hurt them, Ryan, but my animals are very fragile. They are just like people. They need love and care. Do you promise to stop throwing rocks over the fence?"

He hung his head and looked like he was going to cry. "Yes," he whispered.

I felt sorry for him. He didn't know where his rocks were flying. He just liked using his toy.

"But I do know a good place where you can use your slingshot without hitting anything," I told him.

"Where?" he asked as the sparkle came

back to his eyes.

"There's an empty field at the end of the street. It's full of rocks, and I'm sure no one would mind if you moved them around."

"Really?" he asked, ready to go there right away. He suddenly remembered something. "But I can't go there, because Mom has to stay with Gram and Gramps."

"I'll tell you what," I said, putting my arm around him and leading him to the area for the first clue. "I'll take you there tomorrow."

Ryan liked that idea, and so did his friends. I was afraid I'd have seven little slingshotters with me the next day. But I didn't care. A few afternoons in the field seemed a small price to pay to solve the rock mystery.

But that still didn't tell me who had made the complaints. *Maybe I didn't need to know, after all*, I thought. If my pets were safe again and there wouldn't be any more rock attacks, then the animals would be quieter. Maybe the complainer would back down. I was even more confused then about whether to keep my animals if I was allowed, or to let them be adopted by the retirement center.

The rest of the party passed quickly. I didn't say anything to Mrs. Eby about the rocks. I think Ryan was happy about that, because he stuck by my side for the rest of the party.

When the party was over and we were ready to leave, Ryan reminded me about my promise. "Don't forget the park," he whispered.

"I won't," I said. "And I'll talk to your mom about letting you have Lucy."

He gave me his special smile.

"What was that all about?" Joy asked as we walked down the street carrying the remainder of the party supplies.

"I'm going to give Lucy to Ryan. If his mom approves, that is," I said.

"But I thought Ryan was the one throwing the rocks?" Krissy asked. "Do you think he'll take care of her?"

"I think having a pet is the best way to learn to take care of one. Ryan's a good boy. He didn't know he was hurting my animals. He just thought it was neat to watch the rocks fly." I told them about my promise to take Ryan to the park.

"One thing is for sure," Krissy said. "Knowing who was setting your animals off will be a big help when we talk to the Animal Control people on Monday."

Aimee was walking along listening to our

conversation in silence. Finally, she asked, "Why are you giving all your pets away, Linda Jean?"

"What do you mean?" I asked, stalling for time.

"You know exactly what I mean. First you gave Percival to Mrs. Marlowe. Now you're going to give Lucy to Ryan. And Graham said you went somewhere with him the other day, and all he would say is that it concerned your animals."

"What gives?" Joy interrupted.

We were standing in front of my house, so I invited my friends in. Dad held the door open for us as we struggled in with our loads. "You may as well hear this, too," I said to him.

"This sounds serious," he said, following all of us into the living room.

When everyone was seated, I filled Dad in on Ryan and the rocks.

"I hope you explained everything to Ryan," Dad said.

"I did," I told him. "So, now the animals won't fuss, and the complaints will probably stop."

"That's good. It will make our case much stronger in front of the director of Animal

Control," he said.

I took a deep breath. This wasn't easy to tell them. "But even though the complaints might be dropped, I've still decided to give most of my pets away."

Everyone began talking and asking me questions at the same time. I waited until they quieted down.

"Lately it has become more and more difficult to find the time to take care of my animals. Krissy was the first to mention that to me during the museum party. I admit I was angry when she first said that, but I realized after a while that it is true. I love all of my animals, but there are lots of other things I'd like to spend my time doing, too."

"You mean like skating?" Aimee smiled and raised her eyebrows.

"Yeah, maybe like skating," I admitted with a grin. "And there's other stuff, too, like homework, parties, bike rides with Dad, and pizza outings with Mom and her family."

"I'm so glad that you've thought about it so carefully," Krissy said.

"But, Linda Jean," Joy spoke up. "We've worked so hard to win your case so that you wouldn't have to give away your animals."

"I'm not going to give them away to just anyone," I explained. "I'm going to donate them to the Orchid Gardens, the retirement complex. Mr. Rasmussen, the director, said the animals would be welcomed there. That's where I went with Graham," I said, looking at Aimee. "He knew about Orchid Gardens because Nick's grandmother lives there."

Dad tilted back in his chair, and he had a strange expression on his face. It was halfway between a smile and a frown. "What's wrong, Dad? Are you angry at me? I'll pay for the lawyer if that's what's upsetting you," I said quickly.

He raised his hand to silence me. "I'm not worried about the lawyer," he said. "I'm just having trouble watching my little girl grow up."

Eleven

OUR meeting with the Animal Control director on Monday went better than I had expected. Dad's lawyer explained how well I take care of my pets. He told the director how I had solved the problem of the rock thrower and all the noise that had scared my animals.

Aimee gave the director the petition that had been signed by all our neighbors. Joy and Krissy explained that my animals were really important to our Party Time business. They described how excited the children get when they see how friendly the animals really are.

Then Jill Sinclair pointed out that she had found no violations of county health ordinances. She explained that I had a license or a permit for each of my animals.

I found out that Mr. Jambor of Camellia

Street was the person who had complained about me and my animals. He was one of the people who hadn't answered the door to sign the petition. Mr. Jambor works nights, and the animals were waking him up during the day.

I really surprised the animal control people when I told them about my plan to donate many of my pets to senior citizens. I think they had expected a little girl to come in crying about her pets.

But the best part came later that week. Mr. Jambor called to say that he withdrew his complaint. He said he was having a difficult time at work and really needed to rest. He said he was sorry, and that he didn't mind if the animals stayed. I told him about my decision.

That evening, we gave a special party at Orchid Gardens. It was an adopt-a-pet party, which was both happy and sad for me.

"Are they all loaded up?" Dad asked, strapping the last cage onto the back of the pickup truck he had borrowed for the party.

"I'm really going to miss you guys. I promise I'll visit you as often as I can," I whispered as I covered their cages with a blanket to keep out the cool night air.

I climbed into the cab of the truck for the short drive to the retirement complex. Abby followed behind us in the station wagon with the rest of my Forever Friends and Mrs. Marlowe. Graham was meeting us there.

"Are you sure you want to do this?" Dad asked me one more time. "We can still turn around and go home."

I reached over and gave his hand a squeeze. "I know I don't have to give my animals away since the Animal Control officials said I could keep them. But I really want to do this. I know it's the right thing. And it's not like they'll be far away. I can visit them any time I like. I'm even going to ask their new owners if I can borrow the animals back once in a while for the parties."

"I'm sure they won't mind a bit," Dad replied.

"Besides," I said. "I'm still keeping Mascot and Mac. They are enough company for anyone."

"That's for sure," Dad said. "As long as you don't find any more strays with big sad eyes."

"I'll do my best, Dad. But I can't make any promises," I told him.

We drove into the Orchid Gardens parking

lot. A nice, warm feeling washed over me. I knew that my animals would be really happy there. And there was much more open space and fresh air than at my house. A couple of tears rolled down my cheeks. I brushed them away quickly.

Graham rushed out to help us unload the cages. Nick was right behind him.

"I hope you don't mind that I came to help," Nick said to me.

"Not at all," I told him, turning so that he couldn't see the blush beginning to cover my face.

But after a minute I didn't have time to think about anything but finding new homes for my animals.

"I'm Joyce Saltzer," one resident told me. "I'm very interested in a small animal that enjoys being held. I have a lot of grandchildren who come to visit me."

"Well, I have just the right pet for you," I told her, lifting Gertie, one of my guinea pigs out of her cage. I handed the soft ball of fur to the woman and explained what type of food and care guinea pigs need. While I talked, she stroked Gertie's silky fur.

"She's purring," Joyce Saltzer said delightedly, "just like a kitten."

I handed her a piece of paper with the care instructions I'd written out. "I hope you enjoy her."

All around the room, interested residents were peering into the cages.

"To make this a little more manageable," Mr. Rasmussen announced, "we'll have Linda Jean come up here to the microphone and tell a little about each pet. Then she can go around the room and talk to you individually once you've decided on a pet you are interested in."

"This is Harry, and this is Max," I began. "They eat crickets and goldfish. They have to have sun and water, sand and shade, and lots of love."

I walked over to the next cage. "Meet Regina. She's an angora rabbit. She has six babies that all have names and are ready to be separated from her. Rabbits eat rabbit pellets and vegetables, but not lettuce or celery. And this is Oswald. Oswald came to me after he had been in an accident and went blind in one eye."

We spent the evening talking with people, showing them the tricks the animals knew how to do. We told the residents about the animals' daily schedules and habits. The Forever Friends know almost as much about my pets as I do.

A couple of times I looked around the room and saw Graham or Nick or Joy laughing and chatting with a resident. Even though giving my pets away was sad, this was the funnest party ever.

Finally, all the animals had new homes. The residents who had picked pets held them firmly in their laps or on leashes. Or, in Barnaby's case, he was wrapped loosely around the man's neck. I was really glad someone had liked Barnaby. Snakes make great pets.

We packed up and got ready to go.

"Wait, Linda Jean, before you leave," Mr. Rasmussen took the microphone again. "I'm sure everyone here would like to thank you and your friends for your generous donation. I'm sure I speak for all of us when I say you are welcome at Orchid Gardens anytime."

The room shook with the thunder of applause.

"Speech!" insisted Mr. Nanch, the man who adopted Barnaby.

Mr. Rasmussen handed the mike to me.

He nodded his head to encourage me when I hesitated to take it. At first I wondered if I would choke up and start crying. But as I looked around at all the happy faces in the room, I couldn't help but be happy, too. Then I realized that this was a very special occasion.

"First of all," I said. "You're all very welcome. But actually, I should be thanking you. We all have made new friends today—some people and some animals."

The residents laughed.

"My pets couldn't have better homes. And I can't think of a nicer place to celebrate Party Time's 50th party," I said sincerely. "I hope we'll all be friends for a very long time."

About the Author

CINDY SAVAGE lives in a big rambling house on a tiny farm in northern California with her husband, Greg, and her four children, Linda, Laura, Brian, and Kevin.

She published her first poem in a local newspaper when she was six years old, and soon after got hooked on reading and writing. After college she taught bilingual Spanish/English preschool, then took a break to have her own children. Now she stays at home with her children and writes magazine articles and books for children and young adults.

In her spare time, she plays with her family, reads, does needlework, bakes bread, and tends the garden.

Traveling has always been one of her favorite hobbies. As a child she crossed the United States many times with her parents, visiting Canada and Mexico along the way. Now she takes shorter trips to the ocean and the mountains to get recharged. She gets her inspiration to write from the places she visits and the people she meets along the way.